TALL
ENOUGH
TO
OWN
THE
WORLD

14769

BERNIECE RABE

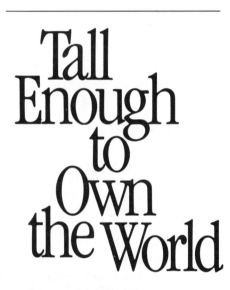

Tall
Enough
to
Own
the World

FRANKLIN WATTS 1989
NEW YORK LONDON TORONTO SYDNEY

Library of Congress Cataloging-in-Publication Data

Rabe, Berniece.
Tall enough to own the world / Berniece Rabe.
p. cm.
Summary: Unable to read, ten-year-old Joey is often in trouble at
school for his rebellious behavior until a series of circumstances
involving a remedial reading teacher, a neighbor, a cat, and his new
stepfather help him come to terms with and conquer his problem.
ISBN 0-531-10681-0
[1. Reading — Fiction. 2. Self-confidence — Fiction. 3. Teacher
-student relationships — Fiction. 4. Remarriage — Fiction. 5. Parent
and child — Fiction. 6. Schools — Fiction.] I. Title.
PZ7. R105Tal 1989

[Fic] — dc19   88-39139   CIP   AC

For Jeremy Rabe,
an excellent reader

TALL
ENOUGH
TO
OWN
THE
WORLD

———————————————

ONE

Mama always made Joey come in through the back door just in case he should track dirt onto their new carpet. Today, it was mud, not dirt, on his pants legs and shoes. He'd gotten splattered good when running away from Mr. Wiley's truck. If only there were some way to get his muddy self, and the note, which weighed heavily in his pocket, past Mama. But let him open the back door and there Mama would be in the kitchen, waiting.

He wished she wouldn't try so hard to be a good mother. "Good mothers should be home when their kids come home," she told anyone who would listen. He was sick and tired of Mama telling Alex, his new stepdad, what a perfect boy he was. He was sure that note in his pocket, though he couldn't read it, told the truth about him.

He cracked the front door to sneak in, new carpets or no.

"Joey, that you, honey?" Mama's pleasant voice had a throaty laugh. People at the beauty shop, where she worked part time, always commented on it.

Right now, he didn't know whether to anwer or not.

His slight pause turned her warm greeting into a sharp command. "Get to this kitchen door, young man!"

If his new dad or his neighbors, the Wileys, showed up this very minute, she'd change. She'd laugh off the scolding. "Kids never do mind," she'd say. But Joey knew she always meant business. He didn't argue. He backed out the front door and ran around to the kitchen door. How can a boy win out against his very own mother?

He kicked off his muddy shoes and jumped inside the back door quickly, for right after they'd moved here she'd caught him outside. Spitting fire about the filth, she'd stripped him right then and there. And she'd stood back and laughed at his nakedness. He'd never forgiven her for that. To this day, he wondered if the Wileys had seen him.

Not surprisingly, Mama was down on her hands and knees waxing the kitchen floor. She didn't believe in the new no-wax cleaners and she waxed often. No one could accuse her of being the poor housekeeper Grandma was. In looks, she favored Grandma, though Mama's stomach was flat where Grandma's was ample and round. Mama's hair was platinum, not white. That long silvery hair swung from side to side in front of his mama's pretty face as she waxed. There was a chance he could get past her without being seen. "Why the front door?" she asked between breaths, not looking up.

"I . . . I didn't want to step on the fresh waxed floor."

"Well, tiptoe. I'm just about finished." She wiggled her shoulders and stretched her back like a contented cat getting up from a nap. She rubbed the last bit of floor.

Joey did a fast, wide tiptoe to get past unnoticed. Sharp smells of wax, hair spray, and herbal essence wafted along with him. Mama draped herself in clouds of herbal essence and pearl jewelry every day of the week.

Just as he was sure he'd made it to the hall without being noticed, there came a threatening cry. "Don't move another inch! What have I told you about getting muddy?"

He didn't move.

"You're not my son and you're not Alex's! You're filthy, like the scum of the earth!" Half dragging, half pushing him to the bathroom, she declared, "My days are hard enough without you adding to it."

"Grandma." He said the word without knowing why he said it.

Instantly Mama jerked him around to face her, and screamed as if she'd been stabbed. "Be thankful I'm not like your grandma! I want you looking decent. I won't let you run loose and ragged and dirty like she let me be. No wonder men never looked at me!"

Joey hated it when she talked like that. He knew it was because his real daddy had run out on her before he was born, forcing her to leave Southern Illinois and go to Chicago for work. She'd had to leave Joey with Grandma.

"I won't have you live or think like your grandma! Not over my dead body! What would Alex say if he came home and caught you dirty like you are right now? He's a decent man. I love him. I want him to have a decent clean kid, a decent home."

Her voice got soft and low for a second. "We're better than your grandma, Joey. I'm not too lazy to see that my kid stays clean. I'll take you to school and bring you home if I have to, just to see that you stay clean." Her voice had risen again until it was high and shrill.

Joey felt like a robot that had been programmed wrong.

"It was an accident. I won't let it happpen again. I'll stay out of the mud. I'll stay clean so Alex won't leave us, Mama. I promise."

Then Joey's mother gave his cheek a pat and laughed with relief. "I knew you wouldn't get all muddy like that on purpose. I know you're starting to do real good at your new school 'cause I get none of those bad notes anymore. Get into the bathroom now and hand me out your dirty clothes. And don't you come out until you shine." She patted his cheek again.

As soon as he had closed the bathroom door, Joey took the note from his pocket, dropped it into the toilet, and flushed. Then he took off his clothes and handed them out to Mama. Carefully, quietly, he locked the door. Mama had forbidden him to lock doors. She was afraid he'd fall into the tub and drown. He was ten years old, for goodness sakes!

He could hear the washer going. His clothes would be clean soon, so Mama was happily singing. He liked her singing. That's why he'd flushed away the bad note—so she'd stay happy. It also left him feeling free after a bad day at school. Just like Mama, singing away her cares after a screaming session.

When he'd gotten that note, he'd felt trapped. So he'd sped away from school—from the teacher who had given it to him—from the kids who asked him what it said. In mid-flight, he'd bent low and scooped up a handful of gravel. Letting the smaller stones sift through his fingers, he'd kept only the largest rock. With one mighty wind up and a great whirl of his body, he'd let it fly. KER-WACK! CRASH! SCREECH! At that sound of cracking glass and screeching brakes, Joey had run for his life. Right through the muddy construction site.

He had cracked the windshield on Mr. Wiley's ancient truck. The Wileys were the best neighbors a boy could ever have. Now, this old black couple who lived just across the alley, who'd liked him immediately, would hate him. Joey wondered if the reason people hated him was because he couldn't read. The Wileys didn't know that about him. He planned to keep the fact that he couldn't read hidden always, even if it killed him.

He eased into the warm bathwater so the pain of being himself might lessen a bit. At least he hadn't cried when Mr. Wiley made his old truck come back, back, back, in an attempt to catch him. Nor had he cried when Mama jerked him around. He used to tell Grandma his fears and let her hear him cry on purpose, so she'd hug him against her big bosom. "Pain drops," Grandma had called his tears. He was too old now to cry. Besides, tears made Mama madder. He'd never tell her he couldn't read. So he guessed the pain would never come up and out of him. He'd never cry again as long as he lived.

Mama called from outside the door as she rattled the knob, "Here's your pajamas. It's too early for bed but put them on anyway. You'll be staying in your room till bedtime. No supper. No television. You're to sit and think about how people like people who look and smell clean. I used Downy Fresh on your pajamas. They smell real good. Joey, open the door! You didn't lock the door?"

Joey had been in the process of quietly unlatching the door and had it open right in the middle of her jerk. "It's not locked," he said and took the pajamas, closed the door and quietly locked it again.

He sponged out the tub with his bath sponge shaped like a Teddy bear with a cake of soap in its stomach. Mama bought that baby thing so he'd use it more often and stay free of germs. Soap bubbles oozed out catching rainbows from the light, just like on television. He was going to miss television. In television commercials, if you get germs, you get sympathy. At home it's get dirty, get yelled at. It made no sense. Joey put some of Alex's aftershave on so he'd smell good and be liked. Then he sprayed some into the air, hoping it would turn the bathroom into a man's room.

Pajamas on, he checked the mirror to see if he was as handsome as his new dad. He was. Two girls at school had told him he was real cute. He sneaked across the hall to his bedroom and hopped into bed. What else was there to do with no television? He lay in bed thinking of his friends, Dirty Steve and Fat Harry. They said they read comics in bed late at night. Sometimes all night long.

He sighed. He couldn't do that. And Mama had put his toys away because Alex was coming home. Joey lay there for an hour or more, listening to every sound. He heard all Mama said during a phone call to a friend. They talked about some movie. About a good place in Chicago to go dancing. About kids driving them crazy.

Joey stared at the overhead light he'd turned on for that purpose. He'd found that, even in the daytime, if he stared at the light, then squinted his eyes tight, pretty and interesting designs formed inside his eyes. This game lasted until his nose demanded he concentrate on odors. Now he lay swamped in a sea of smells, aftershave, herbal essence, laundry and bath soap—and soup.

Mama was heating Campbell's soup or Franco-American spaghetti. He couldn't be sure which. She never went on wild baking sprees like Grandma had done all those seven years he'd lived with her. Mama used the microwave to warm up stuff and the toaster oven to make garlic bread. The sound of the toaster door being shut told him Mama had, at last, put in the garlic bread. The garlic smell rose high, but the sounds stopped for a long while. He tried to shift from smells back to sights and sounds. After all, he wasn't getting any supper. He stared at the light again and squinted his eyes tight shut and listened to the quiet.

He missed the fact that Mama had crept into his room. He didn't realize that until she placed the big panda Alex had won at the carnival beside him. He pretended to be asleep. The quiet was not disturbed at all. Mama switched off the light, but she didn't leave. She just stood there in the shadows by the hall door. The quiet stayed with her. He turned over to face the wall.

Finally, from out of the silence came her whisper. "I wish I didn't have to yell at you, Joey. I wish you'd mind me all the time. My mama yelled at me when I was little. I think I know why I could never please her. It was cause I was firstborn. Now, you're all me and

Alex has got, or will ever get. I want you to know you're loved. I want you to be the best little boy in all the world. Alex'll be so proud to call you his son and I won't ever have to yell at you again."

How could he answer a mama who talked like that?

He nestled down deeper in the green forest of sheets and comforter. He must hide from his soft Mama, standing there in the shadows, saying things that confused him, giving him new secret hurts. He wanted to tell her how bad he truly was and get it over with. How he'd never be what she wanted. His mouth bit the edge of the comforter. Mama disappeared from the doorway. Quiet took over again.

She came back carrying a mug of soup and a bent straw, and placed the straw to his lips. It smelled so good, he sipped, then blew the soup back. "Too hot!"

It was almost dark now but he could still see the little circular waves as Mama blew on the soup to cool it for him. She paused to say, "Once long ago when my mother called saying you was down sick, I came from Chicago and fed you soup through a bent straw like this. You liked it real fine then."

He'd almost forgotten that. She was a stranger to him at that time and it was hard to remember strangers who come and go. This *soft* Mama who sat near him now was a stranger. He felt more comfortable with the hard Mama who usually ruled the roost, as Alex would say.

Just as Joey thought of Alex, Alex's hand popped through the door and turned the bright overhead light back on. He said, "Hey, Chickie, here you two are."

Joey sure didn't blame Mama for loving Alex. Alex's hair was fine and unruly but when he pushed it back he looked just like Elvis. He never wore a hat, not even in cold weather, and he never got sick. Quickly, Alex unzipped and took off the brown suede jacket that showed off his muscles, stuck his thumbs under his broad belt with the giant silver buckle, tapped the pockets of his corduroy pants with his fingers and demanded, "What's wrong? Joey sick?"

"I'm not sick. I just took a bath." Joey spoke quickly, giving Mama time to turn into that special self she reserved for Alex.

Throwing her arms around Alex, Mama added, "Don't you think Joey looks good? And clean? Smell him. You got a sweet smelling kid, Alex. Joey loves the panda you won for him, don't you, Joey?"

Joey was too old for that panda, and Mama was laying the praise on too thick. Her voice was all coated with powdered sugar. She confused him endlessly. He didn't want to answer, so no words would come. He managed to nod and Alex looked pleased.

Alex eased Mama's arms down to her waist and wiggling free, said, "Scoot over, son, I'm with you. I had that truck run to California and back this week. Rough trip. I'm ready for the sack."

Mama appeared shocked. "Alex, you promised me our dates wouldn't stop once we got married. I told you, Joey's all right. Let's make our weekend count, Sweetheart. Have some fun." Her voice rolled and bubbled with those last happy words. "Alex, honey, let's go." She crooned and smiled.

Alex touched her silvery hair and smiled, too. Slipping his suede jacket back on, he said, "I never argue with a pretty woman." Then with an extra big smile, he gave the panda's ear a twist and roughed Joey's hair. "Sure, Joey's all right. There's nothing wrong with our Joey."

TWO

When he got to school on Monday, Joey went to Mr. Orrin's camper truck to use the bumper to wipe mud from the bottom of his shoes. Mr. Orrin was the principal and his truck was first of thirteen teachers' cars in the parking lot. On Thursdays, when the social worker visited, there were fourteen cars. The school bus was parked out of sight, in the garage behind the school, next to the gym.

A sheet of homework came blowing across the schoolyard just as the mud fell from Joey's shoes. Harry, in hot pursuit, was on Joey in a flash, shaking him, yelling, "Darn you! You ruined my graph!"

"Well, why didn't you keep—" Joey started to shout but remembered his promise to Mama to do well at school. He had nothing against Harry. "Sorry, Harry. I'll clean it for you."

"Sorry? Like fun you are. It's ruined. You can't clean it, you jerk. I worked five hours on that graph!"

"I'll make you another one, Harry. I'll make you a hundred. I'm good at graphs. I can do one in twenty minutes flat."

"I'll bet!" Harry put on the earphones attached to his little radio and stomped off in his big waffle-tread boots.

Harry had been Joey's first friend at Woodville School. But just when it looked as if they'd become best friends, Bruce Petz had told the teacher Joey couldn't read. Harry and Bruce were both in Miss Spinner's room. Miss Spinner and Mrs. Pierce were team-teachers when the partition wall was folded back. "I can so read!" Joey had shouted as he shoved a metal desk. But Bruce had nimbly side-stepped. Harry, who was bent over, got hit in the mouth. Harry's smile now showed a small in-verted **v** chipped out between his two front teeth. That caused the first of the bad notes to come home to Mama. Harry hadn't smiled at Joey after that.

"Hey, wait up," Joey called and ran to walk along with Harry to the big double doors of their school. "I really can make graphs, Harry." Harry looked straight ahead.

The rain had cleaned the brick and heightened the school smell. All schools smelled alike. This one smelled no different from the red brick Hill Foundation School, a school for kids who had trouble learning. Joey had gone there for two years after Mama brought him to Chicago. Even the wooden country school near Grandma's where he'd attended first grade smelled the same.

"Do you know all schools smell the same?" Joey shouted so Harry could hear above his radio.

"Yeah, they all stink and so do you, Joey Caruba!"

"Look, I said I'd make you another graph."

"You lie," said Harry, veering out and away.

Joey stopped at the water fountain. He wanted to recharge before going inside. The fountain was one of four at the school that bubbled away constantly. What a waste. Maybe the water was recycled.

Someone pushed his face down into the bubble of water. "Hurry up, Joey. I'm thirsty."

It was good old Dirty Steve, late as usual. Joey moved to one side. Steve spit out his gum into the bowl of the fountain and began a long drink. Joey hoped they didn't recycle the water.

He pushed Steve's head down hard and Steve came up slugging. They both looked up to see Mrs. Pierce glaring at them through the window. Sizing them up. Seizing them with unsaid words.

Joey mouthed the words, "Just funning," and put his arm around Steve's shoulder. Like dancers, they both jumped back as Mrs. Pierce roughly opened the window.

"What was that you said, Joey?" she yelled.

"I said, it's not raining anymore," answered Joey with a big smile.

"Hold the smart mouth, Joey! Get inside. The last bell rang. Do you have a hearing problem?"

That word "problem" knifed him as it always did. Hurt turned to anger. He shot past her window with a leap. He'd leaped like that the time he'd overheard her discussing his "problem" with Mr. Orrin. She'd been his teacher then. It's really hard to fight a teacher who is favored by the principal. Probably because she made the most spectacular bulletin boards in the school. Anyway, he'd found other ways to get back at her for that talk. Two times recently, he'd jumped inside her classroom and said the pledge of allegiance along with her class in a very loud voice. She hadn't dared touch him for saying the pledge.

Just yesterday, he'd pulled faces and done a shuffle dance at her open door when she looked down to call roll. The kids all laughed. That made it even for her allowing Bruce to cut in line in front of him.

He hadn't yet gotten even with her for the time she agreed with Bruce when he said Joey couldn't read. On the third day of school she'd done that. It had ruined what was to have been his new beginnings at Woodville School. He, in turn, had torn up his reading test folder. Mrs. Pierce had said that folder was state property. Then she'd told Mr. Orrin Joey was impossible, and she'd no longer be his teacher.

Well, he was sick of *her,* and was glad to be placed in soft-spoken Miss Spinner's room. Even though being in Miss Spinner's room meant he got to be with Harry and Steve, he had continued to be wild for an entire week. He opened all closed doors. He closed all open ones. He emptied pencil sharpeners on the floor. He did anything to get Miss Spinner to bawl him out. But she didn't. She spoke softly, encouragingly, making it harder still for him.

Sometimes he figured it would have been easier with hateful Mrs. Pierce than with kind Miss Spinner. All the encouragement in the world wasn't going to make him read if he just wasn't capable of doing it. He was constantly forced to pretend to read. It was that or get caught in the truth.

Advancing quickly down the hall ahead of Dirty Steve, he gave a quick leap into Mrs. Pierce's room and pulled loose a tack that held a banner across the top of her perfect bulletin board. He was gone before she saw him.

Steve caught up with him in time so they could enter their classroom together, just in time to see Miss Spinner remove Harry's earphones.

"On your own time, Harry," Miss Spinner said. "Bruce, do you have the folders all passed around?"

Bruce's 100% at the top of every paper gave him all the confidence he needed to march around as if he were a teacher himself. For the last month he'd announced his intention of winning first place in the grammar school science fair. He did experiments with white mice. Joey knew if he could bring Monk to school, he'd win all prizes given for animals. Monk was Mr. Wiley's unusual cat. Monk's mother had been a pure bred Manx with a hard stub for a tail and Monk's daddy had been an alley cat with a long soft tail. Monk had a long, hard tail—a tail like no other cat alive. He looked like no one but himself.

Joey knew he and Bruce looked a bit alike. They had the same small build and the same black hair. Once when they had worn the same navy blue T-shirts with a small green alligator embroidered on the pocket, Mrs. Pierce mistook him for Bruce and was nice before she realized her mistake.

Bruce finished passing reading folders to Violet, to Harry, and to Susan, who sat in back of Joey. Susan always brought hard-boiled eggs with smiling faces painted on them in her lunch. Bruce skipped over Joey and handed a folder to Steve who shared the double seat with Joey. Steve's stomach growled in return and the whole class laughed.

During the laughter, Joey snatched a folder for himself. Miss Spinner opened her mouth as if to speak but didn't. Just then, Steve gave a big lion-mouth yawn. So Miss Spinner spoke to Steve instead.

"Steve, cover your mouth when you—" Her eyes went to Steve's dirty hands. "Never mind. Joey, would

you please turn on the lights. Maybe it will help Steve stay awake."

Joey was up and on the way to the light switch and had just brushed against Bruce when Steve asked, "Bruce, did you skip Joey on purpose?"

"Joey can't—" Bruce began but Joey had him by the little embroidered green alligator on his shirt. The fight was on and his promise to Mama to be perfect was forgotten. The reading period was over by the time Miss Spinner and Harry got the fight stopped. Miss Spinner was dead set against fighting. She could rest during the next period which was social studies. It was Mrs. Pierce's turn to teach.

"We're having a survival film!" came Mrs. Pierce's loud announcement as she pulled back the sliding partition that separated the two fifth-grade rooms. "Line up and go quietly to the audio-visual room and seat yourself on the floor in an orderly manner!"

Miss Spinner didn't have to go with them, but she went anyway. She made sure Bruce got seated on the far side of the room. She sat next to Joey on the opposite side. "Thanks," said Joey and he meant it. He hated to see Miss Spinner work when she didn't have to. From that minute on he meant to make every effort to stick it out in this school and avoid all trouble that might cause Miss Spinner to be sad or for him to get more bad notes sent home to Mama.

He might not be able to read but he loved television and, here, sitting on the floor watching a film, he felt just like his classmates. That is until Bruce read aloud the film title, "Carnivores and Vegetarians." Mrs. Pierce stopped the machine, allowing only the title to stay on the screen until everyone settled down.

Violet had remembered not only that it was film day but also the subject. She had come to school in a yellow dress and yellow tights and was up front showing off her bird. "My yellow canary is a good example of a vegetarian. It eats seeds to survive." Joey yelled for her to sit down. He was trying to memorize how the title words looked.

She sat. But like a flash, Bruce was up running toward the media center and a moment later returned with his dumb white mice to announce how they, too, were vegetarians. He blocked out the title words. It didn't matter. The title words had left Joey's mind completely. Even after Bruce sat down and the film started rolling, his dumb mice cage blocked an entire corner of the screen. It made it truly hard for Joey to keep his promise to Mama and stay quiet and act decent in this school like other students.

However, when gazelles came charging across the screen, Joey had a chance to shout in a nice way. "It's the dry season. They're migrating to get more grass. There's some *interesting* vegetarians," he said.

Mrs. Pierce stopped the film, as she often did, to ask questions. She eyed Joey and asked, "How do you know about the migration of gazelles during the dry season?"

Susan, who'd been scooting around on the floor digging the heels of her Nikes into Joey's backside, said, "He read it!"

Joey smiled as if that were true. Everyone knew that he spent most of his school time doing art, but on occasion, he held a book before his face, turning pages every minute or so. Now, all that had paid off. He pulled a face at Mrs. Pierce's back when she turned to start the projector again. It got the expected laugh—and the expected scolding from Mrs. Pierce.

"Joey Caruba, that's enough out of you." She couldn't have known what he'd done, but added, "And no more shouting out during the film."

She clicked off the lights, and in the hush that followed Joey said loudly, "I didn't say nothing." Miss Spinner's hand shot out and gripped his arm tightly. He'd slipped again. But he'd gotten a second laugh.

It was a great film. Ferocious lions killed zebras. Bobcats preyed on field mice. There were some real neat pictures of men working in a slaughterhouse and later two zookeepers marching up to wild animal cages with big bloody hunks of meat. Circus hands searched for flies and small animals for the snake charmer's snake. A couple of snakes gulped down some frogs, whole. When the lights came back on, Miss Spinner looked a bit pale.

Joey said, "My cat's carnivorous."

Mrs. Pierce ignored his comment and said, "All of you just stay seated for a minute. I have to get this film rewound. There's another class that needs the equipment. If you must talk, talk to Miss Spinner."

Miss Spinner's color returned as she walked to the front of the room and became a teacher again. "Joey mentioned that cats are carnivorous, which is true. They're meat eaters," she said.

Bruce came across the room to say to Joey's face, "You don't have a cat."

"I do so have a cat. He's an interesting cat with a hard tail like a monkey." Everyone laughed—Bruce the loudest.

"And he's solid black and rides between you and that old black man in his old rickety truck." Bruce was mimicking the shaky way of Mr. Wiley's truck.

Before he'd cracked Mr. Wiley's windshield, Joey had often gotten rides to school with Mr. Wiley and Monk, the cat. Now, he must let Bruce believe that there were two cats. His and Mr. Wiley's. Let everyone think Mr. Wiley's cat was solid black. When Joey brought Monk, who really had white splotches, to school, they'd think Monk was his. "My cat's black and white," Joey yelled, wanting it to be so. He took a swing at Bruce.

Miss Spinner was right there between them, pulling Joey away and to the front of the room with her.

Joey shouted, "Bruce doesn't know anything about

my cat! My cat's name is Monk and he's black and white," Joey lied. At the front of the room, he told the class, "I'll bring him to school and prove it!" He didn't know why he had told the class that Monk belonged to him. He tried another swing at Bruce.

Miss Spinner held his arm and demanded, "Why, Joey? Why the violence?" It was almost the same as having Mama call him the "scum of the earth."

"I'm not violent," he whispered hoarsely.

Then she put her arm gently on his shoulder and said, "That film was something, wasn't it? I guess just managing to stay alive is a real victory."

"Yeah," he said. He liked Miss Spinner a lot. But that didn't make him able to read or help him survive in school.

THREE

As soon as they got back to their classroom, Susan scribbled a note and pushed it at Joey. He took it. She stared at him with a fixed smile on her face, waiting. He kept his eye on a pencil that he rolled back and forth across his desk top. She caught it as it rolled off the edge and looked up at him with a spark in her eyes. She probably believed he could read. He'd like to have gotten up and run but she had on Nikes and could catch him. How was he supposed to survive in the midst of a bunch of readers and one of them a girl handing him a note and smiling like that?

He had to open the dumb thing. There was a bunch of writing and two boxes drawn below. Under each box, a word was printed.

"Check one," Susan whispered.

He glared at the dumb thing. She had him trapped.

"Well, yes or no?" Susan stopped smiling and demanded.

He had to check one of these dumb boxes. She still held his pencil. He grabbed a red crayon from the groove at the top of his desk and made a check, then passed it back to her. She looked, then gave him a really super smile that made his stomach flip over. Oh no! It was like those love stories on television, or like when Mr. Wiley teased him about having a wife. Oh no, he didn't want a girlfriend!

To make matters worse, Miss Spinner came up and handed him another note. "Joey, your mother was supposed to have called me this morning. You must make sure this note gets to her."

He wanted to say, Mama doesn't want to talk to you. I can't make her talk to you if she doesn't want to, but his lips couldn't do it. Miss Spinner's look never left him. He said at last, "I can't give it to her."

"It's not a matter of choice, Joey. If you lose this one, I'll be forced to call her. It's for your sake. I care about you. We really need to discuss a few things with your mother." The bell rang for outdoor sports. Joey pretended to read Miss Spinner's note and stuck it in his pocket.

Outside, on the playground, Harry came up to him and asked, "What did that note say?"

"What note? I didn't get any note. Susan just handed me some paper."

Big Harry squinted his blond-lashed eyes, making them thin furry little slits peeping from under his drooping hair. "Susan gave you one of her love notes and you didn't read it? Maybe Bruce was right, you can't read."

"I can read! You saw me read it!"

"Well, stop yelling about it then. Anyway, I wasn't talking about that note. I was talking about the one to your mother. What'd it say?"

Joey was tempted to confess everything to Harry and ask him to read it to him so he'd know what was up. Instead he screamed, "None of your business. I keep what I read to myself."

Harry said, "Last year when I brought a note home, my old man—"

"Who's taking any old note home?" Alex must never see this note, or Mama! "Go wipe your nose, fat Harry!"

Harry's nose wasn't dripping, but Harry's hand went up and wiped it anyway. Then he grabbed at Joey's arm. "You don't aim to take it home! Wow! How do you aim to get away with that?"

Joey moved out of reach, but he liked the way Harry sounded interested and all excited. "I'll manage. I'll throw it in . . . in the sewer!"

"Wow, what'd it say? Tell me, Joey. I won't tell no-body."

Harry had him trapped just as Susan had trapped him. He tried hard to think of something that might sound right, but ended up saying, "I'm not telling you anything, dumb Harry!"

Harry said, "You stink, Joey Caruba!" and walked away.

"I don't stink. Steve's the one who stinks. You stink! I'm never dirty. I always smell good!" There, he'd done it. All in one breath, he'd cut off the only two friends he'd ever made in this new school. Completely exhausted, he collapsed like a parachute onto a piece of concrete jutting out from the broken foundation of the primary wing of the school. He sat motionless. He dared not throw any rocks. He wished Harry would slip in the mud and get it from Mr. Orrin.

Harry didn't fall in the mud. He got back inside the building safely. Joey sat where he was until his strength returned, then spent the rest of the school day in the media center, clear of Harry. Nobody ever got him for spending time in the media center browsing through books.

It was a real surprise when, seconds after the last bell, Harry came running and puffing up to him and asked him in a friendly way, "Hey, Joey, you want to join my secret club?"

"What club?" Joey asked.

"I said a secret club. I can't tell you any more. A secret means a *secret*. Follow me." Joey made no move to follow. "Well, you coming? Joey, you're lucky I asked you. Come on, you going to be a friend or not?"

That did it. Joey followed Harry down the hall. As they got closer and closer to Mr. Orrin's office, Joey had second thoughts and was about to stall again. Harry stopped in front of the room used for music and other special stuff, swung himself through the door, and pulled Joey along with him. The place was piled full of books and there were lots of scribbles on the blackboard. On the desk was a small vase of flowers. Behind it sat an old woman. Harry announced, "This is Joey Caruba, Mrs. Hewes. He can't read."

Terror hit Joey in his heart and in his brain!

"What's going on around here? This is no club! You traitor, Harry! She's a TEACHER!"

Harry was blocking the door with his big body. Joey tried to squeeze past him. Harry bumped him back with a big shoulder. Joey yelled, "Let me through, you creep! You're no friend, you're a dirty double-crosser!"

Harry kept a hard block. "Sorry, Joey, but you can't get into the secret club unless you learn to read."

"Get out of my way, traitor!" Rapidly, again and again, Joey charged Harry. All the while he yelled, "I can read! I can read! I won't let you lie about me. You big fat lying dope! You dope! You dope! You're not my friend!"

Harry didn't use his hands to fight back. He just seemed to push himself up taller with each impact, becoming a giant of an enemy. He reopened the deep wound by standing on tiptoe and yelling over Joey's head, "He says he can read, but he can't, Mrs. Hewes!"

Then he yelled the dumbest thing. "You'll really like him, Mrs. Hewes!"

This rocked Joey so that he felt a great need to catch his wind or die there on the spot—or, worse yet, cry. So he stopped trying to get out the door and just breathed.

Harry then blurted out, "Joey was going to throw a take-home note into the sewer, 'cause he can't read it. He knows lots of answers from television but he hasn't read since school started. He makes trouble all the time. Fights a lot. Won't answer a person. He got a note from a girl and couldn't even read that and everybody knows what Susan's notes say."

Joey reached for Harry's bangs and yanking them, said, "Get that dumb hair out of your eyes. You're seeing things that's not so."

Harry started slugging back this time and Mrs. Hewes pulled him off. My gosh! She was a strong old woman.

She said, "Harry, you'd better leave now. Let me explain things to Joey. This is hardly the proper way to bring your replacement. Gentleness is one more quality I'd like to observe in you before we discuss graduation. But we'll see. We'll see."

Before Joey could move, Mrs. Hewes took his place as guard. He wished for Grandma who never cared if he read or not and who'd always saved him from his young uncle's fists. But Grandma was not here and he was no longer her baby. Not being able to flee like the fast gazelles, he snarled at the old teacher like a meat-eating lion, "Let me out of here, you . . . you TEACHER!"

Mrs. Hewes's voice came to him softly. "I'm sorry about the tactics that Harry used to get you here. Yes, I was a teacher. Yes, the boys call this a secret club and I go along with it. You might call me the initiation to it."

He would have to talk fast. Talking had gotten him out of plenty of tight spots. "You're a teacher, that's what you are! You're no initiation. This is no club!"

"You're bright, Joey. Harry's right, I do like you. Nothing I enjoy more than helping a bright child. And my record of success hasn't been a bad one so far. I'll start by telling you plainly that you can't talk your way past me. Second, I promise you'll learn to read, and very well. That's what brought me back to do volunteer work. I couldn't leave students right in the middle of their progress."

"I don't need your help. I can read. Harry is a liar!" Joey's hands fought themselves; he wanted to hit her but he'd never hit a woman.

"No, I find Harry to be quite truthful. He has other problems perhaps, but lying is not one of them. Believe me, there are other ways to beat this than by lying, Joey." She was talking *into* him, trying to look him directly in the eye but he turned and wouldn't allow it. She kept talking. "I do not judge a person's worth by how much they can read. However, I do need to know where you are in reading. Would you like to show me so we can determine where to start?"

She still stood guard at the door. Maybe he should fight this old lady. She was no Mrs. Wiley or Grandma, and she was asking for it. "No, I wouldn't like to show you how I read! You better let me out of here right now. I'm going home! I'm late already."

"Sorry, Joey. Harry did explain to you that this is a secret club, didn't he? Well, now that you've come to us, you can't leave until we're sure the secret will stay with you, can we? Hush! Hush! Hear me out. Club rules state that no outsiders hear our problems. Harry can be trusted with a secret. He didn't tell another soul that you can't read, did he?"

It was true but Joey refused to acknowledge it.

She continued. "Then you do understand that this session must last until you can trust me enough to take my help. I know you want it. It's awful to be trapped by the inability to read. Right, Joey?"

"Wrong!"

He had to find a way out of this trap of hers. He raged in that little room as if he were a wild animal that had fallen for the bait and had gotten caged. But who would have suspected this plump, short old woman of being a jailkeeper? She looked like a frosty plum with her gray hair and purple clothes. He was trapped among her clutter of books while she stood firmly against the door saying how she wished to help him. Lots of teachers and social workers before her had given him that line.

"I don't want your help! I don't need your help. I'm leaving!" He saw that wasn't enough. He'd have to bomb her with questions. All teachers get carried away when answering questions. Then he could beat it out the door.

He moved to within three inches of her face. "Do you think you can trap me like an animal?" he demanded.

It didn't shake her. She gave a little nod. "You're angry and I can't say I blame you. I'd hoped Harry would explain our process. I'd much prefer you had come willingly. But I can see where Harry had little choice. You wouldn't have come at all."

"Right!"

"Whatever the circumstances, I'm glad you're here. Read a few lines so I know where you are and then I promise we'll move along fast. I don't want you going home late any more than you do."

"What's inside that basket?" Joey shot out the question.

"Why, it's a painting I'm attempting to make of my cat. You like art?" She smiled, a nice friendly smile.

"You know it!" For a moment Joey almost liked the old woman, but not in the way he liked Grandma or Mrs. Wiley. He figured this woman had never made a cookie. Anyway, all that nice smiling and talking would not continue. He inched toward the door. Sure enough, the smile quickly left her face. He must keep her talking.

"I'm leaving." Joey moved.

She spread her arms to cover the entire door. "What are you best at, Joey? Hard work? Laughing? Singing? Talking? I notice you're pretty good at talking. But not reading, right?"

"I'm good at nothing!" Joey backed away.

"Many people think you're dumb, don't they, Joey?"

"They think I'm crazy!" he shouted at her. It was better to say that than admit she was right. If she were Harry, he'd punch her out. But she was an old woman.

"People sometimes call me crazy for doing what I'm doing. They think I should be off traveling all over the world. But I tell them teaching a kid to read is important when—" She stopped.

". . . everyone else can read!" Joey finished for her. Then he realized he'd let himself be sucked in by her. "Reading's impossible!" he declared. Then louder. "Impossible! Impossible!"

"Not quite impossible, just hard work."

"For some people it's impossible! You don't know! I'm not dumb!"

"Oh, Joey, we're all ignorant in certain ways. When it comes to card tricks, Harry can beat the socks off me." She smiled, showing a little flash of gold crown on a molar. Then she held out a little first-grade book invitingly.

Somehow he'd missed seeing her grab that dumb book. She knew plenty of tricks all right. Just like the teachers at Hill Foundation School. They smiled and handed him books. Teachers were all the same. Except at Hill Foundation no one had stood in front of a door blocking the exit. He'd walked right out of that school the same way he'd walked in. By then they knew it was impossible for him to learn to read. But this old woman was blocking the door, smiling, and fast-talking about how possible it was to learn to read. She was really asking for it.

FOUR

Joey spat on the book Mrs. Hewes held out to him. When she jumped in surprise, he made a dash for the doorknob.

WHOOP! Darn that waxed floor! He fell belly down and someone was on top of him, knocking his breath right out of him. Before he could move a finger, he saw heavy-veined old hands grip his own. Good gosh, this old woman had him pinned!

"Get off of me! GET OFF OF ME!"

"Joey Caruba, I won't get off until you have agreed to read for me. I think you're too scared to try because you've failed so often. I *promise* you, you won't fail this time. Don't you see, Joey, that I care for you and every kid like you?" Her hands gripped him even tighter. "I won't let you leave with needless fear still in you! I don't care what or how little you read, but you'll read or we'll

stay here until someone gets worried and comes looking. It's your choice."

She was crazy. He stopped straining. He let his air
go out with a sigh. If only it could be. He took in another deep breath and tried to buck her off, tried to
kick her in the back with his feet, tried to wrench his
hands free. She didn't budge. What kind of old woman
was she? A wrestling teacher? No, she wasn't like
Grandma, but Mama! Mama saying, "Study hard, Joey,"
just as if it were possible for him. He alone knew what
he could or could not do. He struggled harder.

It got Mrs. Hewes some, for when she spoke again,
she was puffing. "I know how you feel. I used to hate
it in church when they'd say, 'Now everybody sing.' I
couldn't carry a tune if it was packaged and had a handle on it. But it hurt so to be left out that I tried, and
the impossible happened. I'm not real good, but I do
sing, and I enjoy it. We'll find out what's holding you
back, Joey, and help you do the impossible, too."

With her last words, her puffing stopped and it
seemed her fingers touched him in a caress. It made
him want to believe. He tensed his back and shouted,
"I been through a million tests. I can't. Get off me. I
hate you!"

She gave a little bounce against his back. "Some
people have grown to like someone they first thought
they hated. I *know* you're not dumb, Joey. You're clever.

Trying to divert me so you could dash for the door-knob! You're smart—a good talker, and you're one heck of a fighter. I do love a good fighter. We'll work fine together. I admire your strength." She had let her hand leave his wrist and touch the muscle of his upper arm.

She was impossible. His body relaxed. Not even Grandma had ever said she admired him. But how was he going to get her off him? She'd probably sit on him until they both died of starvation. He already knew that about her, that she'd never give in. Well, it just so happened that the dumb little baby book in front of his nose was the same dumb book he'd had in the country school when he lived at Grandma's. He'd just begun it, that first year when he'd gotten sick and was taken from school. It was after he'd gotten well that he'd discovered he was not like all the other kids—that he could not learn to read. Nobody had made a big fuss about it until Mama had hauled him off to the Chicago schools.

Joey asked, "You did say I could read as little as I wanted? Get off me and I'll read four pages, but that's all."

Quick as could be she got off him and stood. He remained on the floor, reached out for the book and began to read. "Mother," he said and flipped the page. "Father," he read and flipped the second page. Oh no. A picture of both Billy and Susan and their names was on page three. He'd remembered them as having their own separate pages. There was real reading on page four. He couldn't breathe.

She pulled him up, book in hand, to stand beside her. "Go on,'" she said.

He said, "Billy and Susan" quickly, closed the book and headed for the door.

She grabbed him. "Four pages! A bargain is a bargain." Then with one hand she flipped to page four.

There were four words on that page and he only knew the first one. He'd have to bluff his way. "Billy . . . uh . . . uh . . ."

"Likes," whispered Mrs. Hewes.

It hurt to have her sound so helpful and hopeful. He'd spare her knowing just how impossible he was. Once he got her to say the next two words for him he'd be gone and never return. "Likes . . . uh . . . uh . . ."

Mrs. Hewes flipped the book shut, but she never let go of his arm. "Well, Joey, you can read at least four words, so I guess you're basically honest. I'm strongly in favor of honesty. All learning is based on it. So, we start at the very beginning, do we? That's fine. And so are you. However, you didn't read your fourth page as promised. I'll settle for one short lesson and then you may go."

He gave a hard yank that almost laid her flat, but then helped her regain her balance—he had to in order to hear what she was saying.

"Memorize! Not read but memorize. That's how we'll do it. I memorized piano pieces before I learned to read music. Do you know your phone number?"

"Of course, I do. What do you think I am, a . . . ?"

"All right, I'll ask you to say four lines from this book right after I say them. It's about a stallion that fought the mighty Mississippi and won. He's a bit like you, Joey. You'll love it."

He would not love it. He'd never love reading! When she reached for the book, he reached for the light switch, and then there they were struggling in the dark—slipping and sliding around on the waxed floor. Suddenly, a desk lamp went on. Somehow, she'd reached it. Her hair had fallen loose and was stringing and bobbing as she fought to get a better grip on him, which she did. She looked like a wreck. With her free hand she picked that thin book off the book rack and flipped it open. One day he was going to try to open a book with one hand.

She read, " 'Nothing could stop the wild stallion.' Okay, Joey, say it with me. In pioneer days children read aloud with their teacher."

"Not this kid," Joey began, but was cut short by Harry's voice from outside the door.

"Joey ready to go, yet?"

"All right. I'll say four lines! Nothing could stop the wild stallion," Joey said.

"Fine. Fine." Mrs. Hewes read the other three lines.

"He fought the heat. He fought blizzards. Now he must fight the mighty Mississippi." Joey said them as fast as he could right after her. Instantly, she let go of his arm but kept on talking as he leaped for the door.

"Quite a word, that Mississippi, isn't it, Joey? Those letters look like a row of snakes with little beady eyes. Well, you've done enough for one day. You read well. You have a nice voice inflection. Let's see, this is October nineteenth. By December twenty-second, you can be reading this book. Will you keep this club a secret?"

Harry pushed his head inside. "He will!"

At that, Joey made a run for it. Harry tore right after him. But before they could get all the way through the outside door and get a decent fight going, they were stopped short by a voice.

"Hi, Joey. Hi, Harry." In that little cemented space, walled on three sides by classroom, gym, and bus garage, was Dirty Steve—standing in the rumble seat of an antique car, holding a wire and wire cutters in his hands.

"What're you doing in that car?" Joey demanded. He knew about antique cars. Alex owned models of five such cars. This one was a neat powder blue 1937 Dodge, with its original paint job, but in very bad condition. He'd never seen it around before. Harry picked up what appeared to be an old flannel diaper and began to rub dirt off the fenders.

"It belongs to Mrs. Hewes. She's had it stored in

her garage. But now she's got to use it cause her regular car is broke down. Since she belongs to our club, I got a right to be here in it," Steve said. He snipped around the outer coating of his wire, stripping it clean. "I got more of a right to be here than Harry, even. Eddie and Ernie went back to Texas before they could graduate. I'm the only graduate in the club. I'd be doing my work inside if it hadn't been for your screaming, Joey. Anyway, welcome to the club. You sure fooled me. I thought you could read."

Joey wasn't as set on honesty as Mrs. Hewes. "I can read!"

"No he can't," said Harry matter of factly. "But he will. He's my replacement. Now I get to graduate."

"I'm nobody's replacement! I can read!"

Steve said, "Mrs. Hewes is trustworthy. She won't tell anyone you can't read. We all keep our club a secret. If she says you're smart, you are. I am, too. Did you know I'm building an intercom for our club? Harry thinks you'll keep our secret. Even Mr. Orrin doesn't know we got a secret club right in the middle of his school. He thinks Mrs. Hewes is just a volunteer to help with our homework."

"Harry's a liar! I can read already," Joey lied, then remembered the nice things Harry had said. Still, he kicked the rotten running board of the old car and ran.

"Bye, Joey," Harry called. "See you tomorrow at you

know where. But don't kick Mrs. Hewes's old car. It's going to be my next project."

Joey leaped over the parking lot guard rail. He heard Steve also say, "Yeah, see you tomorrow at you know where."

He ran all the way home, dodging the mud, dodging through the Wileys' backyard to avoid hearing Mr. Wiley mention his cracked windshield. He had thrown the rock, but he hadn't hurt Mr. Wiley or Monk. For a moment when it had happened, he'd thought so. But Monk's cry had been a lot more friendly than Mr. Wiley's. Even now the flick of Monk's tail looked almost like he was waving. Joey waved back. Monk didn't mind being different. He always stood tall as if he owned the world. Monk was his kind of cat. Joey'd tell Mrs. Hewes that he didn't mind being different either. He didn't need her help.

FIVE

That night Joey dreamed that Mama and Alex went to a fair and won him a cat, black with white splotches exactly like Monk. And the real Monk turned all black because of the lie Joey had told Bruce. In the dream Alex had let Joey ride around in the big semi and it was Joey's own cat sitting between them. Alex never once asked Joey to read a road sign. All was perfect in the dream.

It was no fun waking up to find that dumb stuffed panda lying on the floor where he'd kicked it. He ought to take that baby toy and have Mr. Wiley haul it to the dump when he did his trucking work. In a minute, Joey was dressed, had the panda by the ear and was already out the door. The cool air woke him to reality. He'd cracked Mr. Wiley's windshield, so he was in no position to ask favors. To make things worse, Mr. Wiley was outside and had seen him. Joey turned quickly and marched on, out of sight of Mr. Wiley, around to Alex's semi, which was parked in its special driveway behind their house.

He placed the panda on the seat and himself behind the great steering wheel. He drove to Alaska, Maine, Florida, and New Mexico. He drove to Alabama, Minnesota, North Carolina, and Texas. He never had to read a road sign or a menu during any of those trips. He knew the roads by heart. Beside him was his lunch in a black curved-top worker's lunchbucket.

"Going somewhere in a hurry, Joey?"

"Uh, uh, Mr. Wiley! I was just putting this old stuffed panda in Alex's truck so he could haul it off to the dump when he wakes up. I wanted to get the job done before school."

"Hm-m-m. Your dad not rising too early after that long haul last week. He told me he's getting a day's rest time. I myself don't dare to rest. I be going to the dump to see if they got any old windshields, in good condition, what'll fit my truck. Go ask your Mama if you can come ride along with me."

Thinking all would be well if they did find a windshield at the dump, Joey ran in and got a sleepy consent from Mama. She always slept in if Alex had a day off. Then he hopped into Mr. Wiley's old truck next to Monk. Rather than look toward Mr. Wiley, Joey held Monk close. It helped him feel good. So did riding along at a fast clip across a new cut road. The gravel had dried enough that dust flew up behind them. It gave Joey that same safe but dangerous feeling he had while being securely strapped into a fast moving carnival ride. "This is even better than riding behind Alex on his motorcycle!" Joey said.

"Is that a fact?" asked Mr. Wiley. "I do hope there be a glass what fits my old truck. Safety sticker gotta be granted or else no more hauling. As it is, I gotta skip out in the early morning like this so's not to be too noticed by the authorities."

"If you don't find it, tell 'em your windshield was accidentally hit by a rock. They've got to understand and let you do your business."

Mr. Wiley looked at him and clucked his tongue and Joey got a sinking, smothering feeling. He should not have come. He should have stayed in bed. It was too early to be up. He felt like he was cornered by Mrs. Hewes with a reading book in her hand.

Mr. Wiley gave a sad laugh. "Oh, I found a most understanding man. Long as I put something green in his hand round 'side the counter. Whatever, I gotta pay. No one gonna come pay my bills if this truck set idle. Somebody got to make good my windshield."

"I got no job. I'm just a boy. It was an accident!"

"That be true enough. I know you didn't do it on purpose. Hold on tight, we hanging a hard right. Loose gravel, who-e-e-e!"

When they were again on a straight path, Joey said,

"I want to drive a truck like yours, not a big truck like Alex's. You can't go on roads like this with a big semi." There, that ought to make Mr. Wiley feel good.

They rumbled on a way in silence until suddenly a big gash opened up in the earth. Mr. Wiley pulled to the edge of the gravel pit that was turned into a dump. "We'll speak no more till I see if we finds a windshield. This cloud may have a silver lining." There were several old cars and trucks in all stages of rust down in that pit. If they weren't a bunch of rusted battered junk, they'd have been antiques. Some of them still had windshields. Little diamonds of light shot up from them among the dirt and grime.

"Wake up, Monk," Joey said to the cat in his arms. "Let's go look." He put Monk down and they walked near the edge to watch Mr. Wiley in his search. Joey didn't dare go down in the dirty dump to help. Mama would have his hide. After a while, Joey let Monk lead him off near a pond of water where the bulldozer had taken too big a bite. He sifted a handful of gravel, keeping the larger stones to chuck into the water. The rocks felt heavy and he remembered that rock he'd slung so hard, the one that had hit Mr. Wiley's truck windshield. Mr. Wiley was coming up out of the dump already, empty-handed except for a small bent candlestick. Darn!

As if it would undo the fact that he'd broken Mr. Wiley's windshield, Joey threw a rock again in the same manner. But into the water this time, not into the air.

"Why you throwing them rocks so mean? I plum scared to come in range. Good thing I not carrying another windshield. It'd be broke, too. I was sure hoping to find one, to spare you a little money. But we gotta settle this somehow. Come, son, we best go tell your folks and work out some kinda deal! There may still be a silver lining."

"No. No! I'll get a job. Some job that . . . I can't read! I'm too young to drive a truck! Just take me to Grandma's. That's all I ask, take me to Grandma's!" Joey wilted there on the spot into a patch of morning glories, and collapsed in the same way those little flowers did at the touch of the sun. Then he felt Mr. Wiley's soft touch.

"Come on, hop in the truck, Joey. Don't you give up at the mention of a little money. We'll find some kind of job so you can make it right. It's time you get to school now."

Joey raised his head. He opened his mouth. A high-pitched sound escaped. It seemed not to come from his mouth, but out of his ears and nose like a teakettle. "I . . . I can't pay you with no job. Mama wants to keep Alex! I got to be really good for Alex."

"Now, now, lad. You not making good sense. If you wishes me to go first and lay the facts out to your folks gentle like, then—"

Joey bolted and ran and would have gotten away

free had not Mr. Wiley cut through the mud that Joey had skirted around. Joey scooped up some rocks again.

"Go on. Throw 'em, if you think it'll help," said Mr. Wiley.

SPLASH, SPLASH, SPLASH! Joey hurled the rocks into the puddle.

"Whoever you trying to get, I better help too." Mr. Wiley grabbed a handful of gravel and SLAM, SLAM, SLAM, he made fast and forceful work of it. "There. I think the monster of the deep be dead. Tell me what it is you really needs."

"I need Monk. I need to take Monk to school. I told everyone I'd bring him. In social studies, we're studying meat-eaters."

"That be a strange reason for wild rock throwing. I expect Monk will say 'yes' if you asks him. Now hop in the truck, time's a-wasting."

Inside the truck, Joey bent his ear close to Monk and heard his tune. He began to relax in spite of the old truck jolting and grinding its way up Bent Street hill toward school. It muffled what Mr. Wiley was saying.

"I'd say it's not impossible to confide to a friend if you have one, Joey. First, let me confide to you I not only got my sweet wife, but five wonderful grandchildren near 'bout your age what lives way off in Southern Illinois with my daughter. Now, you tell me about your wife and kids."

Joey knew Mr. Wiley was trying to make him feel better. Mr. Wiley knew he didn't have a wife! Joey had another idea. "Take me there. You go visit them and drop me off at Grandma's."

"See? Fancy that! We both got us some folks in Southern Illinois. Sorry, I can't go this minute. You see I got a busted windshield. And, I'm obliged to deliver this bent candlestick to Mrs. Hewes what lives in that big house on the hill. She been decorating it for years with carved mantels, lightning rods, sections of old stained glass that I've drug up and sold to her. She's calls it art. I calls it junk."

Anger flowed back into Joey, making him strong again. "Mrs. Hewes? How do you know about Mrs. Hewes?" She had lied when she said she wouldn't tell!

"Now I shared with you a secret, you tell me your secret what concerns Mrs. Hewes."

"I got no secret about that old woman!" Joey said. He looked about in the truck cab as if to find something to throw.

Mr. Wiley put his hand on the candlestick, and said, "Hold the fire! Hold the fire! I never allow anyone to call my sweet wife an old woman. She be the same age as my good friend Mrs. Hewes. You feel like taking back them words?"

Joey thought of Mrs. Wiley, all curvy and round, with her black face smooth except for wrinkles left by laughter. A woman who wore no apron when she cooked. She had told Joey once she preferred to be charming with a few smudges than hide behind a drop-cloth. Out loud Joey shouted, "Mrs. Hewes is not charming! She's an old teacher who lies, who can't keep a secret!"

Mr. Wiley leaned close. "Mrs. Hewes? Now my Mrs. Hewes never lies. Want to know why I'm taking her this old bent candlestick? She did me a mighty big favor once. Long time ago, she helped my little daughter what couldn't read, learn how. And then, she done the same for me. I got around to owning up that no schooling was offered me as a boy. That I couldn't read to do a written driver's test, when that was made law. I know how she does volunteer work over to that school of yours. I see you was late coming home. And her blue car comes along shortly after that. I put two and two together. Mrs. Hewes don't lie and she holds a secret better than any person near or far."

Joey moaned. So Mr. Wiley had learned to read from Mrs. Hewes! Mr. Wiley stopped the truck with a jerk, just short of home and sat, waiting.

Joey spilled it all, how Grandma screamed when Mama took him away to Chicago, and how two weeks later he'd hit a teacher with a reader and got put into Hill Foundation School. How he was going to have new beginnings in Woodville, but Mrs. Pierce had sent bad notes home to Mama and now even Miss Spinner was doing it. How Mrs. Hewes had wrestled him to the floor.

"I hate her! I hate all teachers!" he said. By the look on Mr. Wiley's face Joey knew he shouldn't have added those words. He'd lost Mr. Wiley as a friend again!

If he wasn't made the way he was, he wouldn't be in trouble all the time. It was reading what was ruining him, driving him crazy! He put his hands over his eyes to close it all out. Over his mouth. Over his ears to shut out his own screaming that filled the truck cab like the sound of yelling in a closed drum. "Don't touch me! Take your dumb stupid cat and his dumb meowing. I hate Mrs. Hewes. I can read! She grabbed me and forced me to read with her. She thinks if she believes something . . . She's a liar!"

Mr. Wiley drew Joey in. "Monk's not meowing. He's crying. Like a boy what's lonely. Me nor Monk never gonna tell your secret. Mrs. Hewes not either. She never told a soul 'bout the time she teach me to read so I can qualify for my driver's license. I know the pain of not reading. Mrs. Hewes does good work helping remedy that. I aim to assist the woman all I can."

"But she sat on me! She sat on me!" Joey wailed into Mr. Wiley's chest. And he stayed there smelling the Irish green soap, feeling the press of hard coverall buttons against his face, taking in solid comfort from Mr. Wiley's arms that blotted away some of his fears.

Finally Mr. Wiley pushed Joey upright and said, "Best I get you home. Now, don't you worry none about hating Mrs. Hewes. My daughter said them very words, too, but she came around. That woman's done found her challenge in you. You lucky to be hijacked and carted away from your fears. If she believe in you, you got ever' right to believe in yourself."

Mr. Wiley saw too much. Joey didn't trust himself. He didn't like it that Mr. Wiley was Mrs. Hewes's friend and on her side, against him. Maybe he wouldn't be friends to anybody, not even Monk. That'd solve everything. He wouldn't have to trust anyone else. How could he even be sure that Mr. Wiley wouldn't tell his secret?

Tapping Joey on the head, Mr. Wiley added, "You got too much functioning in there. You ever needs to talk again, Monk and me got four listening ears and we don't charge too high, does we, Monk? Take this half-breed cat of mine to school tomorrow if you like, Joey."

When Monk made his sound of agreement, which was neither a purr nor a meow, Joey couldn't refuse. He liked it that Monk was a half-breed and sounded strange. From his Manx mother, Monk had gotten the hardness of his tail and from his fly-by-night daddy he'd gotten its length. Grandma had once called Joey's real daddy a fly-by-night. He caressed the full length of Monk's odd hard tail and felt a lot better.

"Monk's different, but he's a fine cat," Joey said. "Everybody in school's going to think so."

"I can't argue that point one bit," said Mr. Wiley.

Joey hopped out then to grab some breakfast, pick up his lunchbox, and face one more day at school.

SIX

Early the next morning, Joey rang the Wileys' doorbell. Then he peeped through one of the little squares in the big front door. Mrs. Wiley motioned him in. "Lands sake child, come in. You come to have breakfast with A. J.?"

"No ma'am. I'm in a hurry. I grabbed a Twinkie. I just come to pick up Monk."

Mr. Wiley's voice rang out from the kitchen. "Monk's finishing his milk, but he's 'bout ready. Got his coat and cap on and his books tied to his tail." Mr. Wiley laughed loudly at his own joke.

Joey wove his way past the large dining room table that was covered with a lace tablecloth. In the center was a round glass lamp with an equally round globe. Both had roses painted on them. He pushed aside big chairs with needlepoint seats. He squeezed past the china cupboard and into the kitchen. He wondered if Monk, drinking milk, had a truly carnivorous breakfast. A

Twinkie was made of wheat flour, so *his* breakfast had been vegetarian. Mama had a strip of bacon, so hers was carnivorous. Alex ate doughnuts, coffee, eggs and bacon and Joey's Cheerios. He didn't know what that made Alex.

"Do you want a ride to school?" asked Mr. Wiley.

"No. No thanks. I want to walk and carry Monk." He cradled Monk in his arms, letting his lunchbox dangle from his elbow.

" 'Course you want to show off Monk to your friends, but if the day gets long, I'll come pick you up."

Joey really couldn't have Mr. Wiley show up for any reason, or Bruce would poke fun at him. "I'll bring Monk home at noon. Look, I'll even leave my lunch here. Miss Spinner let Violet take her noisy bird home at lunchtime. She'll let me take Monk."

"Ha! Monk's got his own noise all right, but he won't cause no one trouble if he's treated decent, will you, Monk? I'd offer to come get Monk at noon but my job won't allow it. We all got to take our jobs serious. Mine's hauling. Monk's is catching mice. Yours is reading. You got business after school. Right, Joey? You take care of it good. The first day's always the hardest. Consider it training. Take good care of Monk."

Joey had skipped seeing Mrs. Hewes yesterday after school. But he didn't tell Mr. Wiley that.

"I'll take real good care of Monk." Joey made no mention of any after school business.

As he left, Mrs. Wiley called out, "Monk, you be-have yourself! Joey, you make him mind."

How could either of them misbehave when they'd be the central attraction at school? Joey walked fast. If this morning went off real well, he just *might* go see Mrs. Hewes after school. With Monk in his arms he felt strong and important, ready to take on the world.

The kids must have seen him coming. Why else would they be all waiting in a crowd at the classroom door?

Joey whispered, "Ready, Monk? Lights, camera, action!"

But they weren't waiting for him and Monk. Bruce Petz was standing in the midst of that crowd, making a speech. "Fifty! That's right, as soon as I breed fifty mice and train them to test out in the maze my dad built, we'll take local, regional and state at the science fair. Maybe even national!"

Joey froze amidst all the ah-h-ing. To his horror, he squeezed Monk too much and Monk made his noise and started clawing to get away. Most of the kids left Bruce and came running. They huddled in so tight around Joey there was no room for Bruce to even look. Harry was saying, "Let me hold your cat, Joey. Mrs. Hewes says I got big strong hands. I won't let him get away."

"No, but you can feel his hard tail," said Joey, stretching his neck to look around, making that a gen-eral offer.

Susan yelled, "Let me be next. I want to feel his tail and see if it feels like a monkey's!" She tried to push in closer.

And Harry kept demanding, "Joey, come on, let me hold him. My old man hates cats. He loves birds and cats catch birds, so he hates cats. What are you going to train your cat to do for the science fair?"

From back of the crowd, Bruce Petz yelled, "He's going to train him to use the cat box! Ha! I know. I'll give his reading workbook to the cat. Maybe the cat can do it right."

A red hot feeling came over Joey. He wanted to yell. He wanted to fight Bruce. But Monk was fighting like crazy himself, still trying to get loose, so Joey's hands were not free. You would think if Harry were a good friend, he'd jump in there and let Bruce have it. No way. Harry just kept on trying to take Monk. It was Susan who finally cracked one of her smily-faced hardboiled eggs over Bruce's head and yelled, "Get lost, Bruce. Joey can do his own workbook!"

"Break it up! Break it up!" It was Mrs. Pierce's gravelly voice dispersing the crowd.

When the space cleared around Joey, he looked Mrs. Pierce in the eye and said, "I'm going to the art room." She never stopped him or hardly raised an eyebrow. Though Mrs. Pierce had insisted that he be given no privileges unless he worked first, Miss Spinner had a rule that Joey was allowed to go to the art room when he wished. It was really an oversized storage closet with shelves filled with art supplies on three sides. Joey kept graph paper and arithmetic papers without words on them stashed in there. Miss Spinner had said, "Art might be the best thing for Joey."

"Please go," Mrs. Pierce said. "And *don't* hurry back."

Bruce yelled, "I'll bet the cat will even have to do Joey's *art.*" Bruce was really spoiling for a fight. Joey had to think hard about the promises he'd made to Mama about being perfect for Alex, and to the Wileys about taking good care of Monk.

When he tried to open the door to the art supply room, something was blocking it. He pushed harder with both hands, only loosely holding Monk. Monk made a jump for it and ran. "Ou-u-u-u." A deep moan from behind the door stopped Joey from chasing after Monk. It sounded like Steve! It *was* Steve lying there on the art supply room floor. "Steve, you hurt?"

"Oh, hi, Joey. You woke me up. Heck, I didn't get to sleep until three this morning. Then Mom drops me off to school so darned early. I snuck in here to catch up on my sleep. Class started?"

"Yeah. But don't go. I want to talk to you. Wait till I catch Monk."

Joey looked down the hall in the direction Monk had gone. The only door open was to the media center, so he went there. The media specialist said, "Why, Joey, you're the first from your class to get going on your assignment. You want to select your books now?"

"No thanks, I'm just looking." That was true. No law said he had to tell her what he was looking for. He walked back and forth, back and forth among the stacks. At this rate, he'd never find Monk. He bent low and started running up one aisle and down the other. Evidently Monk was already good at running a maze. At last Joey saw Monk's tail sailing around a corner. He snatched him and started back toward the door. The media specialist stopped him. "He's carnivorous," Joey said, as if that explained everything. He ran with Monk.

Back among the art supplies, Joey told Steve all about Monk, how very carnivorous he was. Steve acted as friendly as he had after school in Mrs. Hewes's old car. That made Joey feel real good. Then again, maybe Steve was being so friendly just to get Joey to keep the club a secret. Since he'd skipped one day, maybe Steve just wanted to make certain Joey'd go back to Mrs. Hewes. Still it felt really good, seeing Steve smile friendly like that.

Steve stroked Monk's tail and said, "I always wanted a cat. Hey, Joey, you going to bring the cat to club after school?"

So Steve was just being friendly to get him to the club. That was probably why Harry was so eager to hold Monk, too. "No, I'm not going! Not if you paid me a thousand dollars. You can take your old reading club and . . ."

"Harry can't graduate if you don't come back. You have to come back, so we know you'll keep our secret!"

"I can keep a secret better than you ever hope to keep a secret. I've kept one longer than anyone in this whole school. You think you can't trust me? Well, Steve, I don't trust you!" Joey got up as if to leave. Monk was right there ready to get out.

"Aw, you can trust me," Steve said. "Look, I trust you. I just wanted you to come back, that's all." Steve sounded hurt; he didn't sound hateful. Joey looked at him again, good and hard. Just to be sure.

Joey got down two big sheets of yellow paper, one for him and one for Steve. Next he opened a brand new box of wet crayons that looked like paint when they touched the paper. He showed Steve how best to lay out a graph and both set to coloring. Joey moved some distance away from Steve and pulled Monk away.

They'd just finished the graph when some people stopped outside their door and were talking. Joey heard his name, so he put his head against the door to listen better. It was Miss Spinner and Mrs. Pierce. Mrs. Pierce was saying, "I guess one of us better get back to tend the troops. You wait and see what Joey does with that cat. You can't trust him for two minutes. I told Orrin I'd take all the extra duty if he'd exempt me from Joey. I'm afraid I'd use a heavy hand on that kid, if you know what I mean. Orrin knows me. He should forget that psychology stuff and *show* Joey Caruba what's off limits inside the classroom."

Miss Spinner interrupted. "He's called a staff meeting on Joey this afternoon. Joey's reports from his old school finally came in last week. I sent a note home to have his mother attend. He didn't bring in a reply yesterday. Today there's been such a ruckus about the cat, he hasn't had a chance to give me her reply yet. I just can't see using strong punishment, except as an absolute last resort. There are plenty of other things to try first."

Mrs. Pierce laughed. "Neither Orrin nor you will ever get to that little smart-mouthed liar if you don't get tough. Joey *says* he can read because he finds lying easier than working or studying. Let him continue to get away with it and the whole class will be lying up a storm by the end of the year. Thank God, I have him only for gym, films, and recess. What do you do with him all day?"

Joey trembled but did not make a sound. He had to hear Miss Spinner.

"Oh, I think his art is helping him. And maybe his project with the cat for the science fair will . . . I don't know." Just then Monk made his sound.

The handle on the door turned and Mrs. Pierce yanked it open. Miss Spinner said, "Joey! You still in here? Steven, what are you doing here?"

"See?" said Mrs. Pierce. "I rest my case. His influence is already taking hold. Yikes! Grab that cat!" Monk shot out between her legs.

Other classroom doors opened. Teachers and kids poured out into the hall. Mrs. Pierce headed for the office. Soon, Mr. Orrin's voice blasted out over the intercom, "Attention! Everyone back to your seats. It's a simple matter. I'll attend to it. If anyone should see a black and white cat in his room, please report it to me at once. All recess time will be spent outside because the kindergarten is being held in the gym during the repair of their wing—until further notice. That is all."

Right in the middle of the fracas, some men came in through the double doors at the end of the hall, carrying the kindergarten teacher's desk. Joey ran toward them, hoping Monk had not slipped out the door past them. Mrs. Pierce motioned the men on with the desk, caught Joey by his T-shirt, stretching the neck out of shape, and marched him back to his room. She continued to hold him to the spot, in the space where the room partition was partially slid back. He tried to kick himself loose in order to go find Monk. But it meant probable death by strangulation if he moved. Miss Spinner was busy separating Steve and Harry, making Harry return to his own seat. Harry was insisting he, not Steve, should get to sit by Joey and hold his cat when it got found.

Just then, the door opened and the media specialist

said, "Oh, Bruce, I'm so sorry, but something dreadful has happened. I was just taking the new film into the audio-visual room. I saw your mouse cage door open. I think you better come and look. Your mice are gone! Is it all right, Miss Spinner?"

Susan looked at Joey and smiled. He didn't know why. Did she have another love note, or was she glad Bruce's scientific experiment was botched? Maybe it proved the scientific fact that Monk was carnivorous.

Joey decided he wouldn't be seeing Mrs. Hewes today. He'd probably be meeting head on with Bruce. He didn't care. He wanted to fight. He needed to fight. He was a lot more comfortable doing that than facing up to that old teacher who told him to memorize or she'd wrestle him down if he didn't. Face it! He'd never be like Bruce Petz and produce a report card full of straight A's to show his dad.

SEVEN

Miss Spinner's voice sounded tired. "Bruce, go find all six of your mice. Joey, go find your cat. Harry, please go with Joey. The rest of you will kindly open your arithmetic books to page twenty-one. We'll try again to understand the making of graphs."

The cat and mouse situation was getting to Joey, too. He was sure this whole mess had something to do with his inability to read.

Suddenly he felt much better. Miss Spinner was holding up his graph as an example! Even Bruce and Harry hesitated at the door to gawk. Imagine! Joey's work used as a *good* example! It made him burst with energy. Who needed reading!

"Come on, Harry. We got to find Monk. Soon's we get back I'll show you how to make a graph. It's easy." He could have made the same offer to Bruce, but it felt so good to see the sick look on Bruce's face. When Bruce's eyes did meet Joey's, they were fighting eyes, wide and wild and jealous!

Joey pushed Harry to the left. "You look down that hall and I'll take this one."

Bruce beat it toward the media center.

Joey ran up and down the halls. His legs were like the pedals on the generator on "Science At Sunrise" on the Saturday morning television program. But there were no signs of Monk.

The second time around, Bruce met Joey and Harry in the hall. Bruce's face was red. He yelled, "Find that cat, yet? Well, don't worry, Joey, I'm going to find your cat! And I'm going to kill it! It ate my mice! You'll have to replace them or my dad will kill me!" It almost sounded as if perfect Bruce was going to cry when he said the word "dad." Joey was amazed.

"Monk didn't do it. Cats can't open cages. Your mice aren't dead, Bruce."

"Oh no. Well that cat's wild. I say he opened the cage like a monkey does. I know he ate my mice. I found part of one!"

Harry said, "Show me the part you found, Bruce."

"Yeah, show Harry!" Joey had to shout something, fast and loud, because he didn't want Bruce to see Monk. Monk had just slipped into the art storage room, again.

Bruce ran away, but Harry stayed by Joey, still puffing. He said, "Bruce's going up toward the office. Quick, let's check out the primary wing. We have to get organized!"

"Okay," agreed Joey. "I've been there, but double-check. I'll check the hall a second time." Harry started off down the hall himself.

"You're changing it, Harry. Get back here and take the primary wing like you said. And if you see Bruce's mice, grab 'em and put them in your pocket, okay?"

Harry's waffle stompers pivoted and off he went puffing in the right direction. Joey ran down the hall to the art storage room, stepped in, and quickly closed the door. He scooped up Monk and held him close. "You want to get yourself killed? Bruce is mad and you can't trust people who are mad."

He felt Monk's belly to see if it was full of mice. It was trembling. They both were trembling, pretty much. Monk's stomach felt solid enough, no separate little bumps that could be mice. But then Monk wouldn't have swallowed them whole, Joey guessed. Monk was probably guilty. He had to get him out of the art room before some teacher came for supplies. But first, he clicked on a light, grabbed a big, fat, black magic marker and painted the white splotch on Monk until it matched the rest of his fur. Monk's survival was at stake.

"Now Monk, this is an important maze. You and me have got to get through it. All I got to do is get you past Harry and Bruce and Mr. Orrin to the outside of this school. Come on—out the back door of the empty kindergarten room we go!"

Like a fleeting shadow, Joey sneaked close to the corner, then across the hall and into the kindergarten room just after Harry came out, and on to the back door. There he scooted Monk out and whispered, "Go home! Don't stop running until Mrs. Wiley opens the door and lets you in!"

Monk walked a little way and stopped. "Get home!" Joey called as loud as he dared before he had to run back inside. He got back in and out into the hall, just in time to meet Bruce and Harry. "He's not in the hall down this way," said Joey honestly.

Harry said, "I can't find Monk, Joey. Bruce said he wasn't by the office. Mr. Orrin says to come see him soon's we find Monk."

"I'll find him!" declared Bruce. "I won't quit until I find that killer cat! He's evidence for me to show my dad who it was that really ruined my experiment."

Although Joey felt sure of Monk's safety, Bruce's threat still fell like the dull thud of a reader on his desk. It left him suddenly confused and completely devastated. It made him jittery to hear Bruce worry about pleasing his dad. Why Bruce could read, read better than anybody! What more could a dad want?

Clump! Clump! Clump! A construction worker with

big, dirty boots tromped out from the kindergarten room where he'd been working. He said to Joey, "Hey kid, your cat's not going home yet."

At those words, Bruce pushed past Joey and went charging toward the back door of the kindergarten room, knocking blocks aside as he ran. Joey tried to cut him off. Harry tried the same and soon all three fought themselves into a glob as they jammed into the doorway. But Bruce got outside first and yelled, "I-e-e-e-e!" This made Monk go streaking away in the direction of the swamp pool. And all three boys ran in pursuit. Monk was a goner for sure!

Bruce was indeed gaining on Monk. Joey prepared his denial. He'd say that the solid black cat was innocent. Just then, the recess bell rang. About four hundred kids came swarming out all at once and saved Joey from having to lie.

Anyway, it was good old Harry who told the lie, only he didn't know he was lying. He said, "You notice something, Bruce? That cat was all black. Black as night. *Solid black.* I couldn't see a speck of white on him."

"You know something? You're right," said Joey. "It must be the Wileys' solid black cat. Well, we'd better get back inside and look for my cat, Monk. Tell Miss Spinner we need more time."

"Hey, Bruce, you coming inside to help catch Monk?" Harry yelled and pulled on Bruce's arm.

Bruce got a funny look on his face. "Yeah. I guess it must have been that old black man's solid black cat. But what was he doing here, right now?"

"Giving you bad luck, I guess. He ran lickety-split right in front of you." Harry slapped his big hands together to demonstrate. "We got six mice to find, separately or all in one. Get it?" Harry was too jolly. Joey wondered just how much his good friend Harry knew. Still, both he and Harry continued to help in the hunt. And very unexpectedly, Joey found Mrs. Hewes.

She'd just come out of Mr. Orrin's office. Joey came to a screeching halt, then turned and ran the other way. She called after him, "I'll see you later." He didn't answer. He kept running, stopping only to open and close doors. It was good to have the excuse of cat-hunting to do that. He banged the door to Mrs. Pierce's room really loud.

When recess ended the hunt was declared a loss and everyone returned to class. Mr. Orrin said on the intercom, "I hope you've all learned a lesson by this. Cats by nature are carnivorous and nature keeps her balance—some live, some die. It's sad about the mice, but we all must accept the course of nature." Joey thought about how he and Bruce were both fighting to please their dads. And he'd always thought if he could be as perfect as someone like Bruce, that would be the answer.

Steve walked into class ten minutes late. "Boy, there's a black cat down by the pond and it's caught a mouse this long, and he . . ."

"Joey's cat?" asked Bruce. "Was it a white one?"

"Naw. This cat was all black and he was . . ."

"The mouse! The mouse, stupid, was it white?"

"Naw, it was brown. Or maybe—I couldn't tell too much 'cause it was half gone by the time—"

"Class!" said Miss Spinner. "This is school, and I *will* teach! Get out your reading books." Then, for no reason under the sun, she turned to Joey and said, "Joey, you're to go home during lunchtime and report your cat missing and tell your mother that I'm expecting her here, this afternoon. I don't suppose you have a note from her in your pocket."

"Mama works. She told me she can't come until December twenty-second." That was many weeks away and left Joey feeling safe right now. He had his fingers crossed and stuck in his pockets. It was not Mama who'd mentioned December 22, it was Mrs. Hewes. That was the date she'd set to have Joey become a reader. Harry looked at him and smiled, as if Joey had just committed himself to see Mrs. Hewes again.

Miss Spinner scribbled another note, sealed it with scotch tape and handed it to Joey. "I'll expect your mother to answer this in person," she said. Joey didn't need this note business when Monk was on his mind.

He shot out, pushing past Harry and Steve, eager

to get to the swamp. But Miss Spinner chased him down the hall and caught him. What was it with all these teachers being able to catch him? Miss Spinner said, "You're to go home at noon break, Joey, not now."

It'd be a trillion light-years till the noon bell rang.

Mr. Orrin's voice came booming over the intercom, again. "Joey Caruba, come to my office, please!"

Hating the delay for Monk's sake but still feeling like he'd been rescued by Mr. Orrin, Joey went to the office. Slowly. He just knew it had something to do with Mrs. Hewes.

Mr. Orrin greeted him with, "Well, Joey. Miss Spinner showed me an especially fine graph that you made in math. I'm proud of you. I just wanted to get permission to use your graph in a teachers' meeting. Do I have it?"

"If I can leave now to go outside to search for my cat." Why miss a bargaining chance like this, even if you were flattered beyond words?

"It's a deal!" Mr. Orrin shook his hand!

Imagine that! A principal shook his hand, and even gave him permission to leave school during reading hour. Out the door he bounded, filled with energy again.

"Monk!" he called. "Here, Monk! Here, Monk, we gotta get you home."

It took little looking. Monk was by the pond, crouched in a dome of deep leaves waiting to pounce on something. All Joey saw lying there was a scraggly torn chrysanthemum, half covered in mud. Water rippled past it, cutting a little ditch as it made its way into the swampy pool. "Monk, come here!"

Monk didn't come. Something moved under the torn flower. Maybe a field mouse or a water snake. Whatever it was, Monk resisted being picked up. "I gotta get you home. You're not safe around here, believe me. You don't know Bruce Petz. Like it or not, you're coming. I know what's best."

Monk made angry sounds and clawed a bit, but Joey won out. Taking a short cut over what appeared to be dry leaves, but really was squishy mud underneath, he had Monk back at the Wileys in five minutes. He stood at the back door with lots of excuses ready about Monk's delay. But all he did was hand Monk to Mrs. Wiley, who nuzzled Monk to her neck until the cat leaped for his dish on the porch.

"Joey, baby. What's happened to you? Oh, sweet Jesus in Heaven above, what's happened to Monk, too?"

"Bruce's white mice got eaten, so I had to paint his white splotches black. Monk's fine. It'll wear off."

"I guess that makes sense to someone. Well, goodness, child, what about you? You want that neat mama of yours to catch you looking such a sight? You can't go back to school the likes of this. They liable to toss you out. Come in. I'll clean you up."

Joey coughed to relax his throat now that the crisis

was over. He wanted to hug Mrs. Wiley for her kind offer but he just coughed instead.

Mrs. Wiley sang, "If you must cough or sneeze or sniff, be sure it's in a handkerchief." Monk circled in and out around her feet and Joey's, as if dancing to that tune. That set them to laughing.

Handing Joey a tissue and also a big brown fuzzy robe from a nail nearby, Mrs. Wiley said, "First, wrap yourself up, child, then strip off them pants and shoes and socks." She turned her back and faced the kitchen door.

Joey took off the muddy things.

"I do declare, it seems strange to have a solid black cat lapping out of Monk's dish. A. J. will die. What won't you think up next? Lord bless us all, I hope I can scrub him back to hisself again. There's a cold apple-dumpling waiting if you like, Joey."

Later, Joey left Mrs. Wiley's exactly as he'd left for school that morning, except for the note in his pocket. He thanked her for her kindness as his Grandma had taught him to thank people. It occurred to him that he'd never thanked Grandma for keeping him for seven years, nor had Mama. He did not go home to give the note to Mama.

Late in the afternoon at school, he thanked the social worker, or school counselor, as she was called. Because he'd gotten transfered from Mrs. Pierce's room to

Miss Spinner's room, he was required to see a counselor once a week to help him get over his anger at Mrs. Pierce. He didn't mind. He had no problems with the counselor. He was thankful today that she had taken him in early and let him out early.

She answered his thanks with, "No bother. Gives me time to clean away my things before the volunteer comes." The counselor came on Thursdays and saw kids in the same room that the music teacher and Mrs. Hewes used.

Joey, feeling especially kind and grateful, reached out to help the counselor clean up. But, like a flash, the counselor swept her briefcase shut. Too late! He'd seen the folder. On it was a picture of Hill Foundation School and some words were stamped across the top. It must have been bad, for the counselor tried hard to act as if nothing had happened. It was plain that she didn't want him to read those words. Of course, she didn't know he couldn't read. He'd never told her. Mostly she'd let him throw clay at a board to get over his anger at the world.

Now, Joey's chest was afire with anger. No one in Woodville was ever to know about Hill Foundation! Alex must never find out. The note to Mama that Joey had in his pocket surely said something about that report. He had to steal that folder! He grabbed wildly for the briefcase.

"You saw this? I'm sorry. It was my carelessness.

But, Joey, reports do get passed about. They make it easier for all of us to help you—to talk things out. That's all."

"I don't need to talk."

"Maybe next time we could talk about why you screamed at the volunteer reading instructor the other day."

"Mrs. Hewes tell you I did that? That liar!" Joey tried to open the briefcase even as the counselor held it close to her side. But she didn't fight him back as had Mrs. Hewes.

She just held on to her briefcase, opened the door, and said in a soothing way, "Joey, be calm, please. It was Mr. Orrin who told me. We know it has been rough, being forceably removed from your primary home and put into a new place. Not to mention being shifted from one class to another. I'm here to help you clear up the confusion. You don't have to see the volunteer if it makes you so uncomfortable. However, I'm sure she's a very capable person and—"

"And the boy is tired," said a voice from outside the doorway which made Joey jump. It was Mrs. Hewes. Joey didn't like either of them saying what was best for him.

"Of course," said the counselor, looking embarrassed for being overheard. "A little rest can do a lot for the emotions. We were just leaving."

Joey left without looking at Mrs. Hewes. He moved

way to the right as he passed her. But halfway down the hall he stopped. Harry and Steve were there staring him down. It was their way of telling him what was best, but it was different. They were his friends and he did want to be a member of their secret club.

"I don't need any rest," he said sharply to Mrs. Hewes as he re-entered the little room.

EIGHT

Giving Joey every chance to leave, Mrs. Hewes poured some juice from her thermos.

Finally she said, "Hello, Joey. I certainly hoped you'd come back. I wasn't sure. All I can say is I'm proud of you for coming. Would you like a glass of juice? Harry always liked that before we started."

"No. I don't need juice. I'll take the lesson straight."

"All right. I respect your wishes. First comes some work before we do more shared oral reading about that great stallion. If we are going to get down to basics, that means the alphabet. Do you know all your letters on sight?"

Joey didn't want to answer. He felt like running away. He could have. But he thought of the secret club and willed his legs to stay. He also tried to remember all the nice things Mr. Wiley had said about her.

He tried to believe that her being nice, offering

him the orange juice, was not a mean trick to get him to cooperate. It was hard to tell by looking at her face. Layers of rouge piled on top of the wrinkles of her skin. He guessed she didn't look mean, just old.

"Sure, I know some letters," he answered honestly to please her. She'd said all learning depended on it. He didn't plan to lie to her unless he absolutely had to.

She began writing quickly on the blackboard. "Okay, point to the letters you know." She dusted her hand on the leg of her safari pants. She sat back in her old swivel chair like a TV director and waited for him to answer.

He knew A, K, Q, and J. He also knew O and Y. Of course, by admitting he knew six letters, he was also admitting that he didn't know the rest. She wanted honesty. He'd give her the truth. But if she acted shocked or laughed, he'd be out of that door before she could get herself out of that reared-back swivel chair. He found the letters he knew, pointed to them, and said each one. Then he quickly stepped near the door.

She uprighted her chair and he opened the door, but stopped as she exclaimed, "Good!"

He closed the door when she walked to the blackboard. Pecking each letter he knew with her chalk, she said, "You know six letters, that's a good start. Now, I'd like to tell you something interesting about those letters. Listen. The A makes its own alphabet sound in the word *ace*. A lot of letters make slightly different sounds when they are read inside a word. *K* makes the sound 'kuh' like you hear in *king*. *Q* makes the 'qu' sound like *queen*. *J* makes the sound 'ja' like you hear in *jack*."

Joey left the door to look more closely at the letters. How'd she know those had all come from cards? Grandma always asked for an *A* if she wanted an ace, or a *Q* if she wanted him to hand her the queen.

"Joey, tell me a word you've heard the *O* in."

"Cheerio," Joey said automatically. The television commercial flashed into his mind.

"Of course," said Mrs. Hewes. "You'll notice the *O* at the end of the word Cheerio makes its own distinct alphabet sound just as *A* does at the beginning of the word *ace*."

She took the chalk, wrote big *A K Q J O E Y* on the board, and under those she wrote *a k q j o e y*. "There are two different ways to write all letters. You'll learn it in time."

Joey took the eraser and chalk from her. He erased the big E in his name and made a little e. "That's the way I write my name," he said and sat down in a chair.

She nodded, picked up the Mississippi book and scooted a chair for herself to sit right beside him. She read aloud. "The waters were at flood level." He repeated it with her. "They beat Stallion's chest." He repeated that, too. "The waves made Stallion's feet lose hold." After he repeated, she said, "Fine," and closed the book before he had finished looking at the picture. The picture showed Stallion fighting his way through flood waters.

Joey wanted to open the book again. He should have. What she came up with next was unbelievable. She gave him homework!

"Practice at home writing both the large and small letters that you know. Tomorrow, you'll put your finger under the words as we read. That's all for today. Send Harry in."

That was it? The lesson was over! He was so relieved and happy he couldn't move. Finally he said, "I don't do homework. I never have done homework."

She thumped the Mississippi book a couple of thumps and said, "Get Harry. He's around."

"Where?"

"Oh, I'd first look in the clubhouse. He's usually in there with Steve." She was guiding him to the multipurpose room. "This is the clubhouse," she said.

Joey didn't ask the obvious. If she wanted to call the multi-purpose room a clubhouse, let her. He just wanted to find Harry and Steve. He found Harry first, outside, sitting on the fender of the old car. "What are you doing just sitting there?" Joey asked.

"I thought you wouldn't know where else to look," Harry said.

"Mrs. Hewes wants to see you, Fat Harry!"

Harry was up at once and dancing in place. "I'm graduating! I'm graduating. Why else would she ask to see me on your day? She's giving me credit for bringing you in. I got an okay replacement, so now I'm graduating. Don't leave. I don't know how long it takes to graduate, but don't leave!"

Joey laughed. It was fun to see old Harry so scared and nervous.

So, I'm not the only person who gets that way, thought Joey. But he said, "Mrs. Hewes said you better get in there and make it fast, or she'd sit on you." He was teasing Harry the way Mr. Wiley teased him at times.

"She didn't say that! Did she say that?"

It really was funny the way Harry bolted for that door. Joey kept on laughing at Harry until he realized something moved in the front seat of the old car. He froze. He didn't want to be seen or heard like this.

It was Steve's head with its yawning mouth that stuck out the window.

"Harry's graduating," Joey said, relieved.

"You sure? Well, okay. Nobody is allowed to be in there when she gives him the final quiz. We might as well go into the clubhouse and wait. I'm rested up enough now to work on my intercom, I guess. I get to work on it when there's no basketball practice."

Joey followed Steve back to the multi-purpose room. Steve took a key from his filthy jeans. Then he opened a large double door closet, pulled the light cord that dangled at the center, and said, "Here's my electrical stuff."

"This place really is a clubhouse! I thought Mrs. Hewes was lying."

Steve wiped his runny nose roughly on his shirt sleeve. Then he stood there for the longest time giving Joey a fierce look. "She isn't a liar," Steve said firmly.

"I didn't mean it for real." That was the best Joey could do to apologize. He'd had no practice doing that. Not knowing what else to say, he stood quiet like Steve for a few minutes. It could have been an hour though. Then they both spoke at the same time. Stopping, they tried again, both at once. Steve snickered. Chuckles rose from Joey's belly. And soon wild crazy laughter filled the room and bounced off the hollow walls. There Joey was laughing *with* someone! Not *at* someone! They rolled on the floor laughing about nothing until it hurt.

Hurting or not, Joey felt they could have extended that good laugh forever. And would have, if Mrs. Hewes had not come in and said in a serious voice, "Steven, will you get down an armband and present it to Harry, please!"

Steve got up quickly from the floor. He pulled a small stepladder from the closet. From a big rusty hook beneath the top closet shelf, he got down a thin circle of rawhide. All the while, Harry pushed up his left shirt sleeve.

"I am the first graduate to give this to another graduate. Harry, you are now a full member of our secret club," Steve said solemnly.

Mrs. Hewes shook Harry's hand.

Joey's sides hadn't stopped hurting from the laughter. Now they hurt worse from not laughing. From being solemn. From seeing four more pieces of rawhide on that hook and wondering if one day he'd be given one. It was a badge of honor like a patrol belt. Once, when he'd had to sit in Mr. Orrin's office, Joey had tried on a patrol belt. He'd known he'd never be offered that job though.

"Yes," said Mrs. Hewes. "All the rights and privileges of the club are yours now, Harry. You've earned them by diligence and hard work. I'm very proud of you."

Harry faced Joey, waiting.

What was he supposed to do, congratulate Harry? He'd never congratulated anyone in his entire life. He'd never even said the word out loud. Harry kept standing there beaming, looking straight at him. Finally Joey croaked, "Congratulations!" The last part of the word came out as good as the quiz master on a television game show.

Steve went into a coughing fit and then started laughing all over again. But at Harry's sour look he managed to stop. He said, "I'm sorry. I was just happy 'cause I'm not the only real member anymore. Soon as

Joey does, you know what, then he'll be a part member and maybe before long, he'll—"

Mrs. Hewes cut in, "Well, if you're going to discuss the club business, it's time for me to leave. Congratulations again, Harry. You earned that band. Wear it proudly."

As soon as she was out the door, Steve got all businesslike. "Joey, I have to read you the club rules." He took a worn, dirty piece of paper from his jeans and read, "No calling anyone 'dumb,' 'dopey,' or 'stupid.' Always keep the club a secret. Now, we got to test you to see if you can keep a secret. Go on, Harry, tell Joey a secret."

Harry was already sweating and nervous from graduating, but he got even more nervous. Rubbing his bangs back and forth, matting them good where they stuck to his forehead, he finally blurted, "My old man puts white pepper on his grapefruit."

Steve said, "You kidding? How does it taste?"

"How do I know? I don't eat it. But my dad does it everytime I go see him and he said I had to keep it a secret or else. I promised. My mother hates crude men. She don't want me to be like my dad. Steve, 'cause I told it to the club, does that mean I broke my promise?" Harry was rubbing his bangs again.

"No. Telling a secret in a secret club's not the same as telling it around. Okay, Joey, now you have to tell a secret."

"Me?" Joey looked wildly around as if to find something to say. He saw cards sticking out of Harry's shirt pocket. "I play solitaire. She calls me the Joker," Joey said quickly.

"You play solitaire with Mrs. Hewes? She always plays poker with me to help me with my arithmetic," Harry said.

"No. Not Mrs. Hewes, dum—by myself. You never play solitaire with anyone. I sat at one table, Grandma the other. That's when she called me the Joker. I'm a wild player, I guess," Joey boasted to his friends.

Harry said, "It's your turn, Steve."

"Well," began Steve slowly, "I can't tell that I knew all along that the black cat was really Monk. Joey already knows that. Well—" Then Steve's eyes seemed to get bigger and bluer and he whispered, "I love Violet!"

Violet was as soft and pale as the girls in a tissue commercial. And Steve wanted her for a girlfriend?

Harry said, "That all-black cat was Monk? I didn't know that. I saw it with my own eyes. Monk's part white. How could that be, Joey?"

"I'll save that secret for next time. I don't have to tell you everything, Fat Harry!"

Joey wasn't mad at Harry. He was just thinking about the big secret he wasn't telling anyone. It wasn't about Monk. It was: He'd fooled Mrs. Hewes into thinking he was learning how to read, when he knew very well that such a thing was impossible. It would come out someday, and he'd be kicked out, but in the meantime, he got to be in the club.

Joey was happy all the way home. He felt sure he could stay in the club for quite awhile. He'd fooled people for years into thinking he could read and Mrs. Hewes was just a person. For the next three days, he repeated after her the words from that stallion book. She was happy. He was happy.

NINE

All went well for a week. The story was getting so interesting that on his way home, after his session each day Joey relived all the fights Stallion had won. But as he entered the kitchen door the next Thursday, his nose and ears told him something was wrong. He sensed trouble. He smelled cookies! Mama never made cookies. And he heard Alex's voice. Alex was never home on Thursdays and never this early.

He stayed in the kitchen awhile, afraid to go near the voices. He put his lunchbox in its proper place by the sink. Then he took a chocolate chip cookie from the platter, bit off a big hunk and let it go mellow and soft in his mouth. As he bit off the second chunk, Alex's voice came through real loud. "Woman! Woman, you're trying to screw up my life. What for? What for, Chickie? Tell me what for."

Joey rushed to them, but it didn't stop Alex. He

said, "It's a break, I tell you. The job interview went perfect. They want me and my truck, and I want them! It'd mean a move, but I promise you a new house—made just like this one, if that's what you want. Better, even. The houses in Southern Illinois are cheaper. I thought you'd want this. I wouldn't be gone on such long hauls. You'd be near your mother."

"No," Mama cut in.

Alex put out his arm and drew Joey in near. "This boy loves his grandma and needs her. Mr. Wiley tells me how Joey gets so scared when we're out on the town that he has to run to them. Sitting there in my truck thinking about that near drives me wild. I want to spend time with you but I don't want a kid who's afraid of—"

"Joey's okay." Mama pulled him toward her. "He wasn't *that* scared, anytime. He just wanted to be over at the Wileys'. Didn't you, Joey? Joey, answer me." Joey almost choked on his cookie.

How was he supposed to answer that? He knew Mama wanted Alex to think he was perfect. Yet here was his chance to escape reading lessons and get back to Grandma's where reading didn't matter. He swallowed hard. Mama mustn't know he'd taken a cookie without her permission.

"Look at the boy," Alex cried. "He's so scared right now he's choking." He pulled Joey back toward him, but Mama held on.

"I *pay* the Wileys for sitting when Joey goes to their place. Mr. Wiley's got no right complaining about it. I don't neglect my kid, and I don't need any help from my mother. Alex, if you love me, you'll stay right here, and you won't take a job that pays less."

"It wouldn't be a cut really, not with the cost of living less down there. Money's not everything. Let's go down for a weekend and scout around. Maybe you'll change your mind. Anyway, I'd like to meet your folks. And Joey here might like a trip—"

Mama was in such a rage by then and crying and blubbering her words that Alex reached to put his arms about her saying, "Hey, Sugar. Hey, Chickie, look—"

"Don't come near me!" Mama yelled. "Joey's happy like he is. He's been smiling all week long. He's got some new little friends. He even stays after school working hard to do well and make you proud. He sees you plenty. It don't bother him that you're gone a lot. Does it, Joey? Joey?"

It hit Joey that Mama didn't want Alex around him too much. Alex might find out just what an awful person he really was. He stuck his fingers into his ears so as not to hear her, but he said, to please Mama, "I go see the Wileys 'cause I like them." It was an honest answer. And it seemed to please Alex, too.

Alex gave him a slap on the back. "That's good enough reason for me. The Wileys *are* fine people. Say, Joey, how about you going to a movie with me and your mama tonight?" Alex started marching Joey toward the kitchen as if going from the room where their fight had been meant it was all finished.

Before Joey could answer about the movie, Mama grabbed the platter of chocolate chip cookies and said, "I got a surprise for you, Joey! But you don't get any until after you finish your supper."

Joey swallowed deep. "Thanks," he said.

Alex winked at Mama. "But he gets to have all he wants later. Hey, we could take a bag full to the movie. How about it, Sugar?"

Mama smiled and put her arm around Alex's waist. "We could, I guess. But all the movies are rated R or PG. You're home so early. Honey, why don't I put on my champagne dress and we go all the way into Chicago. You've been promising me."

When Mama smiled up at Alex like that, she really looked beautiful.

"Alex, take me to the place where we first met." Then she let go of Alex and ran to the notepad and began to scribble. "Joey, honey, I'll tape the number on the phone. Don't call unless it's a real emergency. Go over to the Wileys if you're just scared."

"I'm not scared of nothing," Joey said, then added, "I could go to a PG movie. I won't look during the bad parts. I promise."

"Atta boy," said Alex. "Why don't we?"

"Alex!" said Mama, "Joey's just a baby!"

So they left him with that insult and a platter of chocolate chip cookies and a glass of milk.

As soon as they left, the house became impossibly silent. Joey almost wished they were still home fighting. He pulled the power knob on the television. The silence exploded into the grand noise of a beer commercial. It lasted through three cookies. He made his alphabet soup last the length of a game show. It could have gone longer but the only whole letters it contained were O, A, and K. Not even enough to make his name. Just a cooked up, broken up mess. Grandma would have taken him to a PG movie, he was sure of it.

Click! Click! Click! Nothing any good on. He settled for a crummy rerun. But halfway through it, he left the television on just for the noise, and laid the cards out for a game of solitare. That kept him busy until the background music on the television got real spooky. He turned around to stare right into the face of a giant earthworm. Worse yet, it had a face on both ends. One male, the other female.

He didn't want to watch it, but he couldn't turn it off and stay in a silent house after having seen that. He watched. Watched it uproot peoples' homes, factories, stores. A little scientist, only one-hundredth the size of the earthworm, tried to kill it with an injection. But it just got wilder, uprooted a long low school, much like

Joey's, its hump breaking the school right in the middle of the multi-purpose room. Then it moved toward a house like the house Joey lived in and—

Joey beat it to the Wileys' backdoor. It seemed he was barely ahead of the giant earthworm!

"Child, child, child!" Mrs. Wiley cried as she opened the door he was practically bursting down. "What is it this time? Why it ain't rightly dark yet and you scared. But come in, come in."

The screen door slammed behind him, making him actually jump into Mrs. Wiley's arms, just as he used to jump into Grandma's when he was scared of the Boogie Man. But that was Mr. Wiley coming to greet him all smiles, and it was Monk touching his legs. It made his world come back into focus.

"Now you just sit here and keep us company while we pop some corn," Mr. Wiley said.

Joey tried to say thanks, but his mouth was very dry. But finally he managed to say, "I guess I could stay a little while. I just came to visit."

"In that case, let's visit," said Mr. Wiley, reaching for his guitar. He taught Joey a couple of chords. They sang a few songs. Mr. Wiley told him not to worry if he could carry a tune or not, just be loud. So Joey was loud.

Much later, Mr. Wiley said, "Who-e-e-e! You done wore me out. You one fine boy, Joey. But us old folks need to go to bed."

"I'm ready for bed, too, Mr. Wiley. See you tomorrow."

So Joey went home and settled into bed with the songs and music still ringing in his head. As long as he couldn't go back to Southern Illinois, it was the next best thing to have the Wileys nearby. He just wished they weren't such good friends with Mrs. Hewes.

He didn't know how long he was going to keep that old woman fooled into thinking he was learning when he wasn't. Nor how long he could keep that same awful secret from Mama and Alex. Sometimes he believed he could do it forever, other times he was sure he'd be caught on the next try. He was too tired to stay awake worrying about it.

TEN

Every afternoon for the next four long weeks, Joey had lessons with Mrs. Hewes. He didn't learn a word. He had her fooled entirely. In other ways, too, it was a wonderful time of year. A time for reading the school thermometer. To call out the temperature loud enough for the whole school to notice him. A time to draw and "color in" a giant parrot poster. A time to see a super film at school on animal mimicry. A time to drink lemonade with Mr. Wiley after helping him plant a new tree. It was Indian summer.

The smoothness of the outdoors seemed to creep through everything.

Alex had begun giving Joey some Kennedy half dollars he found in his change. Joey saved them in an empty olive jar, just the right size. It was his fund to pay for the windshield, though Alex didn't know that. Mr.

Wiley had gotten by with the cracked windshield, so far. But now he had been chosen one out of fifty men to begin a new hauling job, come New Year's. A good windshield was a requirement. Alex thought Joey was saving his money to buy Christmas presents. Joey thought only of New Year's, never of Christmas. December 22, the day he told Miss Spinner Mama would come for a conference, was too close to Christmas. But both holidays were far enough away not to worry. Joey liked things the way they were right now.

Alex took Joey for a ride on his motorcycle. As the breeze touched Joey's bare arms, he pretended he was really the good and normal kid that Alex thought he was.

At school, Mr. Orrin complimented him a little too much on his graph. And Miss Spinner on his poster. But it felt so good that Joey considered doing something else well. Something that required no reading, say, picking the guitar and singing like Mr. Wiley. So far, he'd practiced singing, but that hadn't worked out. And he didn't know how to make the guitar work right either.

He wished he could do it along with someone, like the shared oral reading with Mrs. Hewes.

It never seemed to bother Mrs. Hewes that he was just repeating words she read to him. "Don't be afraid to mimic my voice," she said, and told him again about how in pioneer schools the kids read aloud together.

She even claimed Chinese school kids still did it. He let her be. He'd gotten so good at it that he almost said the words with her instead of after her.

Steve and Harry and he were still good friends and used their clubhouse regularly. It now consisted of the locked closet plus the art storage closet, since Joey had free rein there. They laughed a lot about Bruce moaning over his dead mice. Bruce's dad was trying to get the school to pay for new ones.

Harry had become Joey's bodyguard against Bruce. When Bruce came near, Harry would say, "Belt me one in the gut, Joey. Go on, take a swing!" Joey'd do it and Harry would stand rigid and not blink an eye. Bruce took notice just how tough Harry was and stayed clear. After all, what are friends for? Things went so well for such long periods of time that even Joey's pretending to be normal seemed less pretend and more like the real thing.

In short, for four weeks Joey had been faking everyone out royally. Having good friends like Steve and Harry was worth it. He could keep it up for years if he had to, he told himself. But deep down, he knew that one day it would all blow up.

It happened late one Thursday afternoon.

"Book report time," announced Miss Spinner. "Not everyone has time to read every book. So we'll share what we read. You're to tell the bulk of the story before the class. Then finish it off by reading aloud your favorite passage in the book. Joey, it would be nice if you could have yours finished before your mother comes on December twenty-second."

Miss Spinner made it sound so soon that Joey stormed out of the room. To heck with mimicry! He didn't feel like mimicking normal kids anymore. He felt . . . well, he felt carnivorous, that's what. He felt like biting his enemy. He wished that Halloween wasn't past. He'd love to dress like a vampire.

He did not stop to have a session with Mrs. Hewes that Thursday, but went directly home. The wind was high and sharp, creeping in through the underarm air holes of his raincoat. The whole world had turned cold. It was putting him to a test that he was sure to fail. It was unfair. Unjust. He would not try!

Then why, on the next afternoon, did he stop again to see Mrs. Hewes? He didn't know. He didn't know. He just wanted Steve and Harry to remain his friends, that's all.

Mrs. Hewes never said, "I missed you, Joey." She just said, "You've no need to be upset or worried. Steven has told me all about the book report assignment. Stick with me. Work hard and you'll make it by the time that oral book report is due. I have every confidence in you, Joey."

Joey grabbed at the stallion book. He didn't welcome her talk of the impossible. He wanted only to repeat the now-familiar words that she read. He wanted to be in Stallion's world, not his own.

"One day, Joey, things will all come together and you'll find that you can read. The book you're learning is at second grade level. You *are* learning, you know. And much faster than a second grader because you're older. However, I'll have to ask you not to skip a session again. The boys tell me you've been printing calendars and things at school. I'm pleased. Not only have you learned your letters, but you've found a use for them." She stood for a moment just looking at him.

Well, he certainly wasn't going to try to read in front of his class so that every kid could sit there looking at him. In second grade, when he first came to Chicago, he'd stood before a group and could not read like all the rest. The kids had stared at him as if he were a squished toad on the highway.

He might quit school. He might run away, truly.

On Monday, Joey didn't even stop at his classroom. A short wave to Miss Spinner and he went directly to the art room. He planned to stay there all day. However, when he opened the door, it was to the surprise of his life. There was Steve in a new suit the color of the frosty green mints Grandma kept in a jar. Steve, new and clean, standing there holding a thick cardboard box, the kind that held chalk packed in sawdust. He was stroking something inside it.

"Hi, Joey," Steve said as his two fingers scooped up a naked little mouse. "There's eight of 'em. Their mother is hiding back in here." He paused. "My mother died yesterday."

"Eight of them! Yeah, I can see their mother!" Joey felt alive and happy again as he picked up a tiny baby mouse, its pink skin glowing through white fuzz. "They're going to be white! So, Monk didn't eat Bruce's dumb mice! Here, give me that box! I'm going to—"

Then, Joey realized what else Steve had said. Tears rushed to his eyes. His throat tightened. He didn't know what to say to Steve.

Steve put a chalk-covered hand up to wipe tears off his clean face. Then with a wipe of his nose on the sleeve of his new suit, he sobbed, "I got to leave this school. I can't go back to Mrs. Hewes anymore. My dad just let me come in to get my things and say good-bye before we go live down-home with my grandma. I was waiting for you. Will you tell Mrs. Hewes?" Steve's crying grew louder.

Joey just nodded. Things were way too scary for talk. Steve was being snatched away *to* Southern Illinois just the same way Joey had been snatched away *from* there. Steve had it worse. His mother died. Mothers don't die! Just old people die. Grandma was old. Trying to say something nice, Joey said, "I like your new suit." He touched Steve's arm, and left his hand there.

After a bit, Steve's crying let up. "Dad bought me

this suit at K-Mart last night. My brother got one, too." Steve began stroking the baby mice again. "You'll tell Mrs. Hewes I'll always be part of the club and I'll never tell our secret. These mice can be yours." He handed Joey the box and added, "I hope you graduate." Then he walked away down the hall.

Joey watched as Steve stopped by Miss Spinner and she put her arms around him. Harry would bawl when he found out. He'd better go sit by Harry. Harry and he were the whole club now. Parking the mice on a high shelf, Joey grabbed some sheets of colored paper and ran to Harry. But he didn't get to Harry's seat. He arrived just in time to hear Miss Spinner sadly telling the class why Steve was moving. Joey melted down into his own seat in the front row, the one he'd shared with Steve.

Silently Miss Spinner placed arithmetic workbooks on everyone's desk. She put one on Steve's, and took it up again. Then back down again. Steve ought to be in his place! Good old, dirty Steve, who knew Joey couldn't read and still was his friend. But Steve was clean now, and he was gone. Joey put his head down on their shared desk and moaned as a wild fear grew within. Nothing ever stayed the same.

Miss Spinner whispered, "You want someone to sit up here by you, Joey?"

"No!" Joey yelled and with one great swish he batted Steve's workbook across the desk and on over to

Susan's desk. It knocked all her stuff onto the floor. Kids started jumping up, to see and to shout. Violet, trying to help, made things worse by causing the contents of Susan's desk to spill out. Joey was caught by all that action! He'd always liked a world full of fast action. Fear always left when he was alive and moving! He wadded his colored paper and began to toss it into the air like balls of fire.

"Joey!" Miss Spinner pleaded, "Don't do that. Please behave. Joey! Everyone! Back to your seats!"

Violet bumped Miss Spinner while trying to get back to her seat, causing Miss Spinner to spill the workbooks she still held. Then there was even worse chaos as kids scrambled for them. In the midst of the free-for-all Joey jumped on top of his desk and began to urge them on. "Grab it. Grab it! Grab it!"

"Children, I won't stand for this! Joey," she was pulling at him gently, "I know you've had a hard morning. I'm trying to be patient with you. Get down now and pick up all that wadded paper."

Joey picked it up, and began tearing it into shreds. Miss Spinner's face turned from sad to mad. The room got very quiet. She stormed toward the door, but stopped to say, "I am leaving this classroom for one minute. When I return, everyone had better be working in your workbooks! If I come back and catch any of you out of your seats, I'll . . . I'll . . . I'll . . . paddle you!"

The minute the door closed behind her, Joey

jumped up on his desk, shook his fanny, and jerked his arms in a wild disco dance. The shredded art paper flew from his fingers like confetti. The kids went wild trying to catch it. Some even jumped on top of their desks, reaching and grabbing.

Violet screamed as she ran to the chalkboard, "I'm going to write the name of anyone who's up!" Bruce shoved her to one side and down into Steve's seat. Then he began shoving some boys down into their seats, as well. He yelled, "Quiet! Quiet! Miss Spinner said we had to work!" Other kids sat down of their own accord. Bruce remained standing.

With the room beginning to settle, Joey noticed Harry for the first time. He was sitting at his desk, elbows resting on top, his chin resting on his hands as his eyes glared right through Joey. The heat of that glare made Joey shudder. He had lost Steve. Now, from the way Harry looked so displeased with him, he was sure he would be losing his friend Harry, too.

ELEVEN

After Harry glared at him with such disapproval, Joey had recoiled from being wild and withdrew into being scared and silent.

He'd eased himself into his seat beside Violet just as the sliding door between the classrooms began to open. Bruce dashed for his seat to avoid Mrs. Pierce. Too, late, though. At the very same moment, Miss Spinner had come through the regular door and caught him.

"You need any help in here?" Mrs. Pierce's croak echoed in the silence that followed.

No one breathed.

"No, thanks, I can manage," said Miss Spinner in a voice strangely determined. So Mrs. Pierce withdrew and the sliding door squeaked back in place.

For a long time Miss Spinner stood before them. When anyone raised their hands to explain, she shook her head. Even when Bruce tried to speak out, she shook her head. At last, when attempts to explain were exhausted, she said, "Students, as your teacher, I cannot go back on my word. Bruce, come here."

Then she did an unbelievable thing! She swatted Bruce's bottom one good swat.

Instantly, twenty-seven children began dutifully working in their arithmetic workbooks. Violet was doing Steve's. In a whimpering whisper she said to Joey, "I can't do this problem 'cause I don't know what this word *mills* means."

Joey brushed aside her hand. "It's not *mills,* its *miles.* See, it says, 'How many *miles* to the river?'" HE'D READ A LINE! No, no! He couldn't have. It wasn't possible! He slammed Steve's workbook out of Violet's hands and onto the floor.

In the desktop space where the workbook had lain, Joey saw an inked S + V and under it the word *Love.* Though it was impossible, he knew that word, too. It spooked him. He was beginning to feel wild again.

He grabbed a red crayon from the groove at the top of his desk. But he'd hardly begun a great long fierce scratch through it all when his hand went limp. Then he was crying. Crying because his life had gone strange. Crying for his friend Steve whose mother was dead and who must live with his grandma in a place strange to him.

Miss Spinner was there beside Joey, crooning soft words. But he didn't want *her* words. He wanted to hear his own Grandma, as she spread out the cards, say the familiar words, "Come on, Joey, we'll let the joker be wild."

Taking comfort from those words in his memory, he managed to gain control by the time the recess bell rang.

"You going to be all right?" Miss Spinner asked. "You don't have to go outside. You may sit in the library if you wish."

"I'm okay." Joey got the words out steady enough. But he was afraid to look up and meet Harry's glare again. Or that of the class. They, too, had witnessed his craziness, his crying. He could not face stares or laughter.

But when he did look up, everyone was crowded around Bruce. "How'd it feel, Bruce?"

"Miss Spinner hit hard?"

"You going to report her, Bruce?"

"Show me how hard she hits, Bruce."

Violet sang, "He took it all because of me. Bruce, I think you're wonderful!"

Bruce said, "It was nothing. I didn't feel a thing. You didn't hear *me* crying." He said no more, for suddenly Harry was there beside Bruce.

Harry's head was held low as he tried to get the zipper started in the right notch of his enormous red parka. But his words could be heard quite well. "Get going, Bruce."

One of the other boys said, "Well, I'm going. I'm getting outside before Miss Spinner swats me."

Miss Spinner said, "The sooner we all forget that, the better. Bruce is a fine student and usually very co-operative. But do go outside, and hurry or you'll meet yourself coming back in. Are we friends again, Bruce?"

"Sure," said Bruce as he strode out the door with a following of fans.

His coat zipped shut, Harry demanded of Joey, "You coming outside?"

Joey bounded out of his seat. That meant Harry was still his friend. He grabbed his raincoat and ran to join Harry. They took a different direction from Bruce. Around in back of the school, they sat down on the piece of concrete that jutted out from where the foundation under the Kindergarten was cracked.

"I think I'm mad at you, Joey," Harry said.

A dirty word was printed on the side of the cement. Joey knew what it said! He'd never been sure before. Once he'd pointed out a dirty word to someone only to find out it was the remains of Susan's hopscotch and said "heaven." He touched the dirty word now with the toe of his shoe, motioning Harry to look. Trying to get Harry to change his mood. To laugh as he had these past few weeks.

Harry looked around. "Yeah, I know it's all broken. My dad says the engineers made a gosh-awful mess of this school. What goofs, and them so smart."

Actually, Joey was relieved that Harry hadn't seen the word, or he might believe Joey could read. Joey wasn't ready to believe that nonsense himself. He said, "You got it wrong, Harry. If the engineers were smart, they wouldn't have goofed."

"Mrs. Hewes says people got to make mistakes sometimes to learn. You made a big one just now in class, didn't you? And you're smart, aren't you? Why'd you act like that, Joey? You and me are the only ones left in the club and when Mrs. Hewes finds out what you did today, you'll get kicked out. She may even ungraduate me, and then I'll have to go find a new replacement. And I don't want to find a new replacement!"

Harry was getting increasingly angry as his reasoning took hold. He ended with, "I wish I'd never chosen you in the first place. You started the whole ruckus! Put 'em up, you crumb!" Harry's fists were up already in fighting position and he was dancing an invitation to Joey.

Joey didn't want to fight Harry. So he yelled, "Mrs. Hewes told you to stop fighting. You fight and she'll kick *you* out!"

At that, Harry's fist made contact.

A picture came to Joey in a flash—on television, a karate kick had felled a man twice the size of the kicker. Joey did it! But all that happened was he spun himself around, allowing Harry a good hold on his shoulders.

The karate picture stayed with Joey. Quickly he brought both his arms up and whack, Harry's hold was broken. It worked! Just like on television! Surprised but elated, Joey demanded, "Now you take back calling me a crumb. Promise you won't report me to Mrs. Hewes. Promise you won't get me replaced." He was dancing and doing karate kicks in all directions.

Harry's face was so red his freckles had disappeared. He had his fist up again. Then he grabbed his rawhide armband as if ready to swear by it that he wouldn't report Joey. Joey stood still, waiting. Then Harry's face went all crooked. "Joey, I want you to stay in the club. Steve's never coming back!" Harry sobbed.

"I know," Joey sobbed, too, and the two friends put their arms around each other's shoulders and walked back inside. Harry went to class, Joey to the library.

He helped the media specialist put plastic dust jackets on new books. He thought only of doing the job right and of nothing else. Later, she had him bring his lunch to her desk. As they ate, she attempted conversation. "Keeping things clean makes you feel good, Joey?" she asked.

He knew she didn't mean a thing by that question, but it was a bad kind of question. It carried his mind to other things, to Mama being so clean, Grandma not so clean. Somehow his traveling from one to the other had a lot to do with him not reading! It made him twist and knot in confusion. Made him want to run. Made him want to stay and see Mrs. Hewes again and try the impossible. Reading that line for Violet was freaky. She probably whispered it to him first. And that dirty word on the cement, maybe he'd always known it. Anyway, this pile of new books before him had millions and trillions of words in it. It would've been better if he'd known no words at all. That way was familiar. He'd know how to act.

"Would you ever try the impossible?" he asked the media specialist.

"Of course not, Joey. But putting dust jackets on this amount of books is quite possible, though I do make a goof now and then." She put some mending tape over a tear.

But his mind wasn't on her chores. He had to get out of this world. He'd take Mr. Wiley up on that offer he'd made just yesterday. "You ever needs a thing, remember I be your friend, Joey." Well, he needed to be taken back to Grandma's, where reading was not the center of life.

He tried not to think of people that he'd miss, like his friend Harry. He'd known all along that one day it would all come to an end. There was no sense to getting in any deeper. If he stayed, even Harry would expect him to keep trying.

He put plastic covers on books the rest of the afternoon. It was a long slow job, but that was okay. It gave him time to think up just how to get Mr. Wiley's help without argument. At the sound of the last bell, he dashed out of the building and went straight to the Wileys'. First, he'd insist Mr. Wiley make good his promise to be of some help. Once he got Mr. Wiley to nod his head on that, he'd state what sort of help he wanted—a ride to Grandma's! Back where he wasn't expected to keep trying when things got too painful. He wouldn't tell Mama he was leaving because she'd try to stop him.

TWELVE

The old truck was in the Wileys' driveway, as if waiting for Joey. Mr. Wiley was at his workbench, attached to his garage. Joey rehearsed what he was going to say as he ran. "Mr. Wiley—" he began before he'd come to a full stop.

Mr. Wiley scrubbed hard on a handsaw with an oily polishing rag. "Got to get these protected from the weather. Got just a little leeway. Don't start my new job till New Year's and I gotta get my other jobs and chores done first. I'm thankful for that grace period to get new glass in my windshield. What brings you home this time o' day, Joey? I thought you been staying after regular to be with Mrs. Hewes."

Joey frowned. Mr. Wiley's words had stopped his planned speech. But he helpfully picked Monk up from the workbench so Mr. Wiley would have a place to lay the newly oiled saw.

"What kind of answer is that? Frowning? You get ready to talk, I'm here. Meanwhile, I got to give a few more things a bit of spit and oil. I sure do feel fine knowing my new job means steady work, year round. Man my age! Who-e-e! Hey, Joey, why you not talking? You wanting something? I can't know, unless you open your mouth and makes it known."

"Take me to Grandma's! Right now!" There, he had said it. Not nice, the way he'd planned, but he had said it. Mr. Wiley could not say no. He'd promised.

"Hold on, Joey, you got me looking outa too many windows at one time. I didn't hear you say you was running away, did I? Leaving Monk and me? And how about that tree you planted? You got to be around come spring—see it take on new life."

"Mr. Wiley, I don't want to talk about it. You promised if I ever needed something—well, I need you to take me to Grandma's."

Apparently, Mrs. Wiley had overheard. She came running out into the yard and enfolded Joey into her arms.

"Just a minute," said Mr. Wiley as he pulled his wife away. "Joey wants to tell us something what's bothering him."

"No I don't! I just want you to take me to Southern Illinois. *Please,* Mr. Wiley. Right now. I got to go!"

Mr. Wiley rubbed his chin. "It be a mighty long

ways to Southern Illinois. Gas costs a pretty penny. Trucks need to stop at weigh stations for inspections."

Joey's despair turned to anger. He squeezed Monk too tightly as he yelled, "Just take me, *now!*"

"Joey, I couldn't do that. First off, I got a cracked windshield that'd never get past them inspectors in case I got pulled over on a long drive. Second, don't you think we ought to speak to your mama and Alex?" Now he was putting his arm on Joey's shoulder.

Joey wrenched free. "Liar! You promised! You promised!"

Mrs. Wiley began to pull at him roughly, and gave him a little shaking. "Joey, we are your friends, definitely, but land's sake, child, you just come on inside and let—"

"Let him be, Sweetheart," Mr. Wiley said. "Let me handle this. Come on, Joey, hop in the truck with me. This be the tail end of Indian Summer, not a bad time for traveling."

That was more like it. Joey took Monk and climbed into the truck cab. Mr. Wiley kept pushing around in his tools a bit, hanging up the oiled ones. Joey wanted to tell him to stop fooling around and hurry it up, but he thought it best to not say anymore.

Mr. Wiley held up a piece of wire and called out, "One more minute. That gravel pit's been rough on this old truck. 'Bout time I laid into me a new job. I got to be up bright and early of a morning. This new job requires this old truck be shipshape and I be punctual. But it's worth being punctual for. No more spot-work hauling. A lasting job. It's worth getting things shipshape. Got to fix this dangling light or police won't like it. Might stop us and ask questions. It's bad. Even tied on tight, we won't be able to drive no one-eyed truck after dark."

Joey knew that Mr. Wiley was politely saying they could never make it to Grandma's by dark. Joey fought listening. It would be go now or go in December. For sure, he'd have to leave before that book report was due on December 22. As Mr. Wiley had said, Indian Summer *was* a much better time for traveling. More than that. Now was when Joey's mind was set. He didn't want to give it any chance to weaken. He got out to watch Mr. Wiley wire the light. "Could I help?" he asked.

"Nope," said Mr. Wiley, giving a hard twist on the wire with his pliers. "What you planning on using for food on this trip? Would you want to get a little lunch from your Mama?"

"I won't get hungry," Joey answered. Then quickly, so as to cover the fact that he was leaving without Mama's knowledge, he added, "No one should have to eat if they're not hungry."

"I hear you, son, but I plot my course on set meals." Mr. Wiley hung up his pliers. "You thought this leaving business all the way through? Your leaving home now could possibly be a move in the right direction. Or, it could be a bad move that's going to stay bad—even if you changes your mind later. What do you say?"

"I say let's get going." Joey answered quickly.

Mr. Wiley jumped up into the truck bed and began bouncing around to test things generally. "Them teachers at school, what's been working so hard with you, they gonna miss you," he said as he bounced.

Joey knew stalling when he saw it. "Mr. Wiley, don't you know I'm sick of school and sick of teachers? I already quit. I can't go back."

"Don't talk down teachers. We have teachers all the days of our lives, first your mama and daddy, or your grandparents. Then after your schooling, life goes right on telling you new things. Schooling helps. Ask a man what never had the privilege." Mr. Wiley jumped down off the truck bed and landed with a finger pointing at Joey's chest. "You, Joey, has got to face up to facts."

"I have. I am who I am!" Joey got back into the truck cab.

"You leaving? Hey, wait for me!" Mr. Wiley said in his teasing voice and hopped in alongside Joey. "I know you be who you be. And you a good boy. I know what's troubling you. Reading. Son, I never had the chance to get that tool. It took some doing, but I saw my daughter had a chance. I wishes it was in my power to see all boys and girls, black or white, get the chance. It's precious. Give the thing time. Your spit never gonna be good enough without it." Though Mr. Wiley had let those stalling type words spin out, he had started the motor and the truck was soon rolling. Slowly they crept along the same street they'd once taken on an early morning to the gravel pit. Now it was a tarred city street, not a graveled road.

The tar on the street still looked new, slick and molten, flickering in the afternoon sun. It took them five minutes to make it one block. "This new street head south?" Joey asked.

"It do. I reckon it do be heading south. It'll swing around so's you can say good-bye to your school what you won't be seeing no more."

Mrs. Hewes's old car sat in that little sheltered spot between the office wing and the bus garage. Joey looked the other way and saw something he hadn't noticed before. He said, "Look. The thorn apples are still on the tree and the leaves are all gone." It was the sort of thing Mr. Wiley usually pointed out to him.

"Pretty sight. Birds will make short order of them come winter." Mr. Wiley was interested and he kept driving. Joey knew how to make polite talk as good as any adult.

He deliberately picked a wise statement to start Mr. Wiley preaching and keep him driving south. It was something Miss Spinner had told the class. "Birds fight over cherries, but they won't eat some red berries, like those over there."

Mr. Wiley picked up on it, just as Joey knew he would. "That reminds me of something! Yep! And you got to see this. Wouldn't have you leave us and miss it!" Mr. Wiley stopped the truck.

Darn! It had worked all wrong. Mr. Wiley was out and had run around and was opening Joey's door.

"Be fast, Joey. Come with me. I hope they still there." Mr. Wiley pulled Joey out and Monk followed.

It was an apple tree in the corner of someone's garden that Mr. Wiley forced him to see. "Look! Look up there, Joey! Prettier than them thorn apples. Right?"

Joey wished he'd never started these dumb nature talks. He backed away from where Mr. Wiley had dragged him and tripped on a garden hose. Mr. Wiley obligingly helped him right himself and pointed at the apples in the tree top. They were huge, round, Roman apples. All hanging like Christmas tree bulbs among the leafless branches. It was a pretty sight. "Dumb," said Joey. He forgot all about polite talk. He resented Mr. Wiley interrupting their trip.

Mr. Wiley's old arm stretched until he was able to reach an apple. His old hand cupped gently around that apple and down it came. "Here, Joey. Careful, son, hold it easy. You can study it in the cab. We got us a long trip to Southern Illinois."

Joey was only too glad to go back to the truck. The apple he held was hollow. The birds had pecked clean the insides. Just the skin and the core were left. It still looked perfect if held high, as Joey had to hold it in order to get into the cab.

Mr. Wiley said, "That apple wouldn't keep a doctor away. It needs doctoring." Then he laughed and shifted a lot of gears. "It be a fooler all right. Not worth picking. Not like you, Joey. I figure you still a good solid apple. Truly worth something. I do hate to see you running from a little hard work. Mrs. Hewes not been all that hard on you, has she?"

"You drove a truck for years without reading," Joey said.

"True, but every year they put up more and longer road signs. I'm mighty thankful to Mrs. Hewes I can read them. Look at that sign right there!" Mr. Wiley screeched to a stop next to a sign that had the letters S T O P on it. Another sign nearby had lots of writing but Joey refused to look at it. As he turned his head away, he thought he heard Mr. Wiley switch off the ignition. There was no need for that at an intersection. It was the intersection not far from school. They'd hardly gone any distance at all!

Joey was sick as could be of all this polite and fancy talk. And he wasn't going to let Mr. Wiley stop to teach him any more lessons! "Hit the gas, Mr. Wiley! We're past the new tar. Let's go!"

Mr. Wiley tapped the ignition key with his finger. "This truck motor done died. It read that sign what said stop. I don't think it's going to start up again until we do some long hard talking, friend to friend."

Quick as switching to a new television channel, Joey had the door handle down and was jumping out. "I hate you! You're not my friend! You're playing tricks on me. You hate me, Mr. Wiley."

Then Joey was running, running, running! He'd run all the way to Southern Illinois if he had to. Monk evidently had jumped out with him and was running along, cutting in front, thinking it was a game. Behind him Joey heard Mr. Wiley's truck following. He cut across people's lawns where the truck could not follow, down near the swamp pond on the lower end of the school grounds. That did not stop Mr. Wiley, however. Soon Joey heard his familiar call of, "Monk, pr-r-rurt! Monk, pr-r-rurt! Monk, pr-r-rurt!" He had gotten out of his truck and was in pursuit on foot.

"Monk! Go back to Mr. Wiley! You can't come with me. You're his. Go!"

But Monk was still leaping from side to side, having fun. Joey, taking in Monk's frolic, caught a glimpse of Bruce coming across the schoolyard. To avoid Bruce and to save Monk, he had to get the cat in the direction of the Wileys' house. Get Monk near enough to his home and he'd make it to safety. It meant cutting through the mud, but Grandma wouldn't care. That's where he'd be tonight, with Grandma, not Mama.

Split, splat, Joey kept running. He kept calling to Monk to follow. But Monk, still playing, took to the tall grasses. Joey followed. He couldn't just run away and leave Monk to Bruce. Though the blades cut and scratched his ankles and hands, Joey continued to run after Monk. Out of breath at last, he stopped and yelled at Monk, "Oh, why don't you just go home! Git home!"

Instead, Monk came toward him. Joey scooped Monk up and said, "Monk, you don't want to run away with me. You're not mine. You belong to Mr. Wiley." He sat down in the tall grass and held Monk close, his breath coming out so hard it made little waves in Monk's fur. Suddenly the tall grasses parted. An angry yowl rose from Monk, and there was Bruce, wildly swinging his lunchbox. "You ate my mice! Killer!" Bruce struck with his lunchbox, but Joey had tossed Monk out of danger. Or maybe Monk had leaped away.

"Bruce! Don't you hurt my cat! Monk, dodge! Git home, Monk!" Joey had a hold on Bruce's jacket but one jerk from Bruce and the hold was lost. The next sound was the lunchbox making contact.

Monk flopped over. No weird non-cat sounds anymore. Silence. Total, awful silence. Monk just lay there in the bent yellow grasses as if asleep and sunning. Monk was dead! Joey froze. He could not even cry out because he refused to believe what he saw. Life left Joey just as it had left Monk. Monk was dead because he had followed! That was too much for Joey to bear.

It was Bruce who moved, dropped his lunchbox and was down on his knees begging. "Get up, Cat. Please get up, Cat! I didn't mean to hit you. I really didn't mean to hit you."

Mr. Wiley, who had taken a less direct angle in the chase, came in closer. In a polite but puffing voice, he called ahead to Bruce, "Thank you. Thank you for catching Joey's cat. Monk never had a habit of jumping outa the truck before. Now this makes the second time, thanks to Joey Caruba. A man my age having to—" Then he saw Monk and dropped down to cradle him close, put his ear to him. He finished in a husky voice, "Joey, we better be taking our cat back home."

A weird sound followed. At first Joey though it was Mr. Wiley giving way to grief, the way he himself wished to do. But it was Monk's sound. Monk was alive! Joey began to shout it. "He's alive! Alive! Monk's not dead!" Another voice joined his. Bruce Petz and Joey Caruba were shouting the same thing!

Mr. Wiley was smiling broadly, sharing their happiness and his own. At last, Mr. Wiley said, "It's 'most suppertime, Joey. Your mama gonna be worried sick something's happened to you, too. You like to ride along home with me, hold your cat on your lap? I can't hardly hold him myself and drive." Joey was lost for words, but of course he would. He nodded.

Bruce, too, did not speak. He stood there looking scared as they left. Later Joey looked back from the truck window and saw Bruce slowly walking away. The wind was sweeping leaves all around his muddy shoes.

Joey asked Mr. Wiley, "You remember that garden hose I tripped on? I need to hose the mud off my pants legs. Mama hates mud."

"I hears you son. I hears you."

Monk began purring to Joey's stroking. Mr. Wiley reached over and stroked Joey in much the same manner. Joey said, "Steve's mother died and he left for Southern Illinois this morning. I cried in school today. I'll never learn to read. I didn't mean to cry. They weren't bad tears like Bruce said."

"I know, Joey, they washing tears. They keeps the inside strong."

THIRTEEN

At the apple tree, Joey had offered to wash some of the mud off Monk's feet as well as from his own, but Mr. Wiley shook his head. "Cats what are bathed by others gets so they won't preen or clean themselves."

"I'll walk the rest of the way," said Joey and Mr. Wiley left for home with Monk sitting tall and looking out the window as always. Mr. Wiley never looked back to make sure Joey followed. Joey appreciated the trust. He wouldn't be running away anymore. And he'd try not to scream or lie anymore either.

Mr. Wiley beat him home and when Joey arrived, Alex had just walked away from talking to Mr. Wiley in the driveway. Alex put his arm around Joey and said, "Well, son, I guess we all just got to take things one day at a time."

Mama was on the steps and heard. "What does all this mean?"

"It means hot chocolate, and maybe some pop-corn," answered Alex.

It meant, of course, that Mr. Wiley had told Alex something. Joey never found out what, nor did he ask. He just enjoyed hot chocolate and the popcorn that Mama popped and had a good time playing Star Wars with Alex. He'd never played that game and he'd gotten it last Christmas. He couldn't read the directions and he'd had no partner anyway.

On Sunday it really turned cold enough for hot chocolate. Still, Alex took Joey for a last motorcycle ride before winter.

On Monday morning, snow came. It sat in little cotton puffs atop Mr. Wiley's picket fence. The cool silent snow suited Joey fine. It covered up the mud. It made everything clean. It cleared the mind. Joey was ready to deal with Bruce's mice.

Harry stopped him as he got near the school to say that the garage mechanics had insisted Mrs. Hewes leave her old car in the bus garage when it snowed. They were lovers of antique cars, just like Harry. "Now, our club even includes the bus garage!"

What did Joey care about that? He'd be out of the club anyway. He pushed on past Harry and the line of kids by the school door, went directly into school and on to the art closet. From the chalk box on the top shelf he took out the mice. Five little ones went into his left pocket, the mother and the other three babies in his right. He pushed some sawdust on top so no heads could peek out. Then he went back outside.

When he got down by the pond, he looked for a decent shelter so the mice would not be left out to freeze. There were some deep footprints frozen in the mud, but not deep enough. It was a chore, but with a broken stick he dug a sufficient hole into the side of a dirt mound. Into it he put some dry seed-filled grasses and on that the mice and the sawdust. So Bruce's science project was returned to nature. They would live. He didn't want the mice dead anymore than Bruce had wanted Monk dead.

Once the score with Bruce was even, the next person on Joey's list was Mrs. Hewes. Since he'd decided against running away, he'd have to tell her, right after school, that he was quitting. All day he sat at his desk drawing. When kids made remarks about his wild dancing on desk tops last Friday, he just pressed the crayons harder, but he didn't speak. Finally the last bell of the day rang and Joey went slowly toward the reading room. He wasn't mad enough to go with speed.

In the hall, Harry grabbed him again, bunched up the front of his coat and held him against the wall at arm's length. Harry's arms were longer than Joey's. "I don't aim to fight you, Joey, 'cause I don't want to get kicked out of the club. And you better not get kicked out, either, you hear me? And keep your hands off my project! I oughtn't to even told you where it was."

The pressure Harry put on Joey made him good and mad, but what Harry said last left him too surprised to scream. He stopped struggling to say, "Some project? I wouldn't touch Mrs. Hewes's old car."

"It is some project and you know it. Else the mechanics wouldn't let her have a space in the bus garage. It's a priceless antique and they want it to stay nice, just the way I do. But they wouldn't bother it, so it had to be you that was fooling around with my—Mrs. Hewes's car."

Wasn't this something? Now that he'd really started to care about rules, he'd gotten falsely accused. "Harry, I didn't touch Mrs. Hewes's old car, honest. I've never messed with cars. You sure you didn't do it and forget?"

At that, Harry let go of Joey's coat. "If you didn't polish her car, who did? Come on, Joey, I'll show you what happened."

It was nice to have Harry believe him, at last. He guessed he could delay seeing Mrs. Hewes for a minute. Anyway he needed time to think what to say to Harry, too, about quitting the club. But as they ran through the snow to the bus garage, Joey only thought of how cold it was and not of excuses.

In the bus garage, Joey wondered why Harry was so angry. The car looked great. The trunk and all the outside plated pieces shone bright from being polished. "See," Harry said sadly, "that was my job and someone else did it! I'm sorry I thought it was you, Joey."

Touched by Harry apologizing so easily, Joey tried it, too. "I'm sorry that you thought it was me, Harry. It had to be the mechanics."

A glow lit up Harry's face, the melting snow on his eyebrows sparkled and he said quite loudly, "It's okay this time, Joey, but those mechanics better never do it again!"

The mechanics across the garage never paused. But Joey heard a noise close by. "Sh-h-h," he said and pulled Harry down beside the old car. "Someone's over there. I think we're being watched."

A voice from the corner said, "Calling Mrs. Hewes, calling Mrs. Hewes. Over and out." It was Steve! He was sitting on the dirty floor in a suit that already looked gray instead of frosty green. He'd been gone only three days, counting today. A brand new green, orange, and red stocking cap was perched on the back of Steve's matted black curls.

"Steve!" Harry and Joey said together. Then Harry added, "So you're the dirty sneak that's been doing my job!"

"I had to do something, Harry. We got back this afternoon and I didn't want to start school till tomorrow. Dad's out getting his old job back. Unemployment's high down home. Listen, my intercom's working!"

Mrs. Hewes's voice, sounding a bit gratey, came through, "Steven, Steven, is that you?"

"It works!" shouted Steve as he jumped around a few times. "Did you hear her?" His smile grew wider and wider until he could hardly talk as he called back to Mrs. Hewes, "It's me. My intercom works!" and switched it off.

An intercom was a pretty nice invention, Joey guessed. Steve couldn't get enough of back-slapping and congratulating. Joey did his part of it, too.

"Well, boys. This is more like a club. Steven, I hope you're back for good. And welcome back to you, Joey." It was Mrs. Hewes, come to join them.

Steve said, "Yes ma'am, I'm staying."

"I'm glad. The intercom works very well. Congratulations! And congratulations to you, Joey, for coming back. I suspected on Friday that you'd decided to quit. But that's neither here nor there. The important thing is that you've returned. It takes twenty times the courage of coming the first time to return after one has quit. Well, come along. There is work to be done and time to catch up on."

"Mrs. Hewes, I was just coming to . . . Steve was messing with Harry's project. I mean . . ."

"I wasn't messing!" Steve said defensively. "I was keeping busy till club time, when I could show everyone my intercom. My dad says our family's got to keep busy so's we won't miss my mom so much."

"Your father is wise, Steven. And I'd like to discuss

your intercom at length, and we will, later," said Mrs. Hewes. "Joey, coming?"

Joey followed her back to the reading room just as if he'd meant to do it all along. They started right in with the shared oral reading of the stallion book, Joey following along with his finger and saying the words just a shade behind her. It was almost as if they were reading together. Then right in the middle of one page, Mrs. Hewes suddenly stopped. Caught off guard, Joey shot on to the next three words before he could stop.

"Well," said Mrs. Hewes. "Well, I thought so! You're reading! I had suspected you'd started to read. Many people quit just as it becomes evident they're winning at a thing." She began to dance in a little circle, much as Steve had done when his intercom had worked.

"I'm not reading!"

She stopped her crazy dance and looked at him directly and said, "Joey Caruba, you are indeed reading. All this practice and word attack and knowing letter sounds is cumulative. It's beginning to make sense for you, much in the same way babies sometimes suddenly start talking in complete sentences. You are reading! Let's get on with it and you'll see for yourself."

He didn't wish to put it to the test. If he wasn't, he couldn't bear it. If he was, he couldn't bear that either. "I don't know why you're dancing like that when you don't know what . . . I ought to know if . . ."

"People dance for different reasons. I hear you did a bit of dancing on top of a desk last Friday." She said no more but turned to the reading, "The blizzard was intense." Joey joined in. She never stopped again to make him try it alone, except when it looked like Stallion was going to be killed. He grabbed the book from her then and read the next line, alone.

"Well," said Mrs. Hewes.

Joey just grinned and grinned and grinned, until his feet caught the action and he was dancing.

"Well," said Mrs. Hewes, "what do you have to say now?"

Joey stopped dancing and collapsed to the floor all weak and sprawling as a dropped handkerchief. "I'm glad I stayed to see Steve's intercom. I'm glad you made me read. No other teacher could." He thought that answer might please her. He wanted very much for her to be pleased, but she wasn't.

"I didn't make you! No one is ever *made* to read."

"Lots of teachers tried. But I couldn't do it. It was impossible. I know you made me read that first day. You sat on me." He still had not entirely forgiven her for that.

In defense, she grabbed him again, in much the same way Harry had grabbed him and pinned him to the hall wall. "Oh yes, and I yelled at you. And I will do it again if I need to, to wake up all the energies within you! You're a child with too good a memory and ability to waste! Look, I had to let you know you're not the same little kid anymore. You're ten years old, a fifth grader! It was time for you to erase that garbage!" She let go of him. "Tell Steve he can come in now."

"But I'm not telling him . . . I'm not telling . . . you know what." He couldn't bring himself to tell anyone that he'd actually read aloud. "It might go away and I won't be able to do it again."

As he went out the door he heard her say, "I rather doubt that."

FOURTEEN

As Joey went out into the garage to tell Steve that he could come in, he began to tremble. He couldn't share his triumph as Steve had his achievement with the intercom. That intercom of Steve's could work in front of anybody. Joey could never stand in front of his class and read aloud on book report day. Anyway, when you thought about it, reading one line was hardly reading at all.

He found Steve still by the intercom and said, "Mrs. Hewes says you're next. I don't know why she couldn't have just told you on your old intercom. I don't know why she had to ask me to send you in."

"No problem. I'll use the intercom to tell her I'll come."

While Steve was doing that, Harry hardly acknowledged Joey. He was balancing on the running board of Mrs. Hewes's old car and polishing the top. His hand moved as fast as blades on a fan. "Pretty, isn't it?" Harry finally asked proudly.

"It'll do," Joey said.

"It's great! Say it's great, Joey. It shines like layers of glass. I do a good job. My old man says I have strong hands. What's eating you now, Joey? Mrs. Hewes get on to you? You still afraid to admit you can't read? Well, I admitted it right off, on the very first day."

"Okay, I can't read! There, I said it. You happy?" Joey felt good saying that. Always before, he'd die rather than say that. But now, it was a relief to say it.

Harry called to Steve, who'd just finished his intercom call to Mrs. Hewes. "I made Joey say it. He just told me he couldn't read. I've known it all along." Harry began polishing again.

Joey snatched his rag and threw it on top of a bus. "You didn't make me say it. I said it myself. Anyway, I *can* read!"

Steve said, "It's all right if you can't read, Joey. You don't have to get so mad about it. It don't make any difference."

Joey yelled again, "I *can* read!"

Why didn't they dance for him and congratulate him?

Harry was climbing on the hood and reaching on top of the bus to get his rag. Having got it, he stood up there, as if on a stage waving a flag, and announced, "Joey, you're lying. You can't read! Why do you always have to lie? You got honest once, keep it that way. Oh nuts, go home, Joey!"

From across the garage, a mechanic yelled, "Don't stand on the hood of that antique car!"

Harry jumped off his stage and went back to car polishing.

Joey made a grab for the rag again. "I can read, Fat Harry!"

Harry's strong hands were bunching up the front of Joey's coat again and the two began going around and around.

"Calling Mrs. Hewes, calling Mrs. Hewes. Joey's out here saying he can read! Joey and Harry are fighting. Over and out. Roger," said Steve into the intercom.

Both Harry and Joey stopped to listen to Mrs. Hewes's reply. The raspy voice said, "I refuse to speak for Joey. Let him speak for himself. Over and out to you, Steve. Will you please come in."

With both boys glaring at him, Joey said once more, "I can read!" Then he stalked out into the cold.

Outside and quite exhausted, he leaned up against the brick wall of the school on the part still warmed from the afternoon sun. But now it was snowing again and getting dark early. He watched the snow fall. Felt it on his nose. Stuck out his tongue to catch a flake. He and Mrs. Hewes knew he could read! He whirled with the snowflakes for a moment. Then he headed down his street for home and was met with the startling sight of Christmas lights. Mr. Wiley and three other houses on the street had turned on Christmas lights!

He could forget taking one day at a time, and December 22 was coming up fast. How awful to be frightened and excited at the same time.

Mama went bowling soon after Joey got home. He didn't practice his reading. Instead he took a piece of black art paper and punched pin holes in it and held it up to the light so that hundreds of little stars danced about the walls. In the primary grades, teachers gave stars to the best readers. At first he felt he deserved those stars. Then he wadded the paper up and threw it away as he'd done the notes to Mama. So what if he could read one line in the stallion book and one line in an arithmetic book? Bruce could read the encyclopedia.

Joey ate some soup and watched television. But the fact that he'd have to read several pages come Christmastime kept creeping in, taking over. He went out the back door, away from the Christmas lights, and stood for a while in the dark and let the cold snow hit him in the face. He was Stallion battling the blizzard. Piercing snow hit him from all angles, trying to get him to forget about reading. Stop trying.

Suddenly the snow stopped, and it was still light. Very light. The light of the setting sun danced along on the snow's brilliance. Joey felt it was dancing for him—because he had read two lines. That gave him courage and he held his head high like Stallion, like Monk. He could see for a thousand miles. He could live through a blizzard, he could live through that book report, too. He felt like he owned the world! He stood looking at the dancing lights until the chill chased him back inside to snuggle under his comforter and fall asleep.

But in his sleep there were no dancing lights. The blizzard pelted Mr. Wiley's old truck until his windshield cracked in a million places. Two giant windshield wipers could not wipe the cracks away.

When Joey awoke, he thought he was never going to go to sleep again until that book report was done and over with. He dressed rapidly for school. First, he stopped and checked Mr. Wiley's windshield. There were no new cracks. Mr. Wiley even said he might be given a short extension because of the difficulty of finding glass for a truck as old as his. He surely hoped so. He surely hoped all went well with that new job coming up. Joey wished for a silver lining for Mr. Wiley's windshield.

When he got to school, he pushed his hands against the wall, as if he could break it down. Impossible! Schools would always be there, standing solid. Teachers would always be there demanding book reports in front of the class. It's a thousand times harder to read before kids you want for friends than for an old teacher in private.

During class, Joey stuck to art projects. He showed his graph to Susan who said it was interesting. He needed that compliment. But Violet reported to Miss Spinner that Joey was making his graphs all wrong.

Miss Spinner said, "It may not be according to the book but it's an imaginative new approach. Mr. Orrin showed one at teachers' meeting and the teachers were impressed."

That was more like it! Joey checked to see if Steve and Harry had heard that. They had. After school, Steve reported it to Mrs. Hewes on his intercom. "Joey can make graphs good, even if he can't read."

But Joey was reading—right along with Mrs. Hewes. Each day he dutifully followed a second behind her words. But regularly she would stop short and he'd read on. Line after line, before he, too, stopped. He guessed he was ready for such tests. As more and more houses lit up on his block and all through town and kids talked of nothing but what they'd get for Christmas, Mrs. Hewes said, "There's no doubt about it, Joey. You'll be ready on the twenty-second."

She drilled him hard on his sounds and made him write his letters on the blackboard. Once, he even corrected a mistake she had made! Mrs. Pierce would have killed him for that, but Mrs. Hewes said, "Thank you. Thank you very much, Joey. A teacher can have no greater compliment than her student's excellence."

Joey kept that compliment. He also kept the chalk he made that correction with in his pocket as a trophy. And each day he'd take the chalk from his pocket and write the word STALLION on the blackboard at the beginning of each session. Mrs. Hewes was pleased. "What an excellent note to start on, Joey!"

At the *close* of each session, she was not so pleasant. She'd say, "Tonight I want you to read, read, read. Homework will make you a winner. Don't look up from it even to think or talk or anything. Television must not be turned on for the duration. You have a deadline to make and if you'll just concentrate on reading and nothing else, the time will go fast and you'll make it."

At least part of what Mrs. Hewes said was so. The days passed swiftly. While other kids complained that Christmas was too slow in coming, Joey said, "Too fast!" He'd dutifully taken the Stallion book home each night in a paper bag, read in it, and brought it back to school again in the paper bag hidden under his jacket. Once, Mama came home from shopping and had caught him reading. She didn't say a word. She didn't even act as though it was an unusual practice. Just teased him about him not knowing what she'd bought him for Christmas. In a way, that was good.

Alex was a different problem. Joey just couldn't refuse Alex's first offer to take him along on a short haul in the semi. But he brought along his stallion book and tried to sneak a peek by turning his back to Alex. He got awful sick and they had to stop for him to vomit. Alex said, "You should never read while riding." When Mama heard about it, she said she figured Joey was coming down with something. Maybe he should stay home from school for a day. But Joey couldn't afford to miss a session with Mrs. Hewes. He swore he'd only vomited a little and Alex did not contradict him.

But once Mama caught him reading by flashlight after he should have been asleep and threw a fit. "Joey, too much reading will make you sick. You'll ruin your eyes. Watch television and give your eyes a rest. You're going to know that book by heart!" She took it out of his hand and looked at it, then laid it down. "Oh, about horses," she said and walked away, uninterested.

After that, he was forced to watch television until he was in the house alone. And, of course, he could not read at school and let the other kids see it was a second grade book he read. Still he worked harder at this reading than at anything he'd ever done in all his life. There was no way Mrs. Pierce could say, as she once had, "Joey Caruba, you're just lazy!" Maybe he was beginning to believe, as Mrs. Hewes believed, that it was possible for him to read in front of the class on December 22.

He was too busy to have time to be scared when he was alone, so he never ran over to the Wileys anymore. But one night he was reading about a trader lying about Stallion's ownership. He put down the book and ran to Mr. Wiley and said, "I'm sorry I lied about owning Monk."

"There, there. There be no need for you to tell me that, Joey. But I accept your apology. I know how much

—145—

you love Monk and that's a natural sort of ownership. And Monk approves."

"Thanks," said Joey and to everyone's surprise returned home at once to get back to his reading. Nothing could stop him!

At home, he locked the doors, taking responsibility for his own safety. It was a new and good and scary feeling, to know he'd not ever have to run to the Wileys again. From now on, he would only go to visit. Every night he did just fine, until the night before December 22.

He couldn't read. He couldn't read at all that night. The words were forgotten as soon as they left his mouth. The sentences had no meaning. If he stopped to take a deep breath, he couldn't even find his place to start up again. He finally gave up. If he went to sleep, the morning would come all the faster. That's what he'd always been told about the night before Christmas. He needed the rest, badly.

But sleep was wasted. It did not come in one great lump. It came in bits and pieces. He woke up maybe thirty or forty times. Neither mind nor body rested. He felt like a toy top that was beginning to spin down only to be jerked awake and rewound. Then off he'd go again screeching and reeling across the night of troubled sleep. Mr. Wiley had once told him to look for the silver lining. Well it must be the lack of nightmares. That night he never slept long enough to have one.

He felt cold but Mama wouldn't allow the heat up for she was conserving energy. The cold never left him, not even when he put on his down jacket the morning of the twenty-second. But nothing must stop him.

However, he was stopped, by his first mistake of the day: he ate. He promptly vomited his Cheerios. But he didn't tell Mama for fear she'd make him stay home, though truly he wanted to do just that. But live or die, he would face up to this tough test. Face it as Stallion had faced his.

A lot of honking made him look to the sky for the familiar V-formation of geese. But it was Mr. Wiley, offering him a ride. Mr. Wiley knew about this day, and his offer was appreciated, but Joey waved him on. In doing so his book fell from his jacket front into the wet snow. He picked it up, brushed it good, and secured it in place again under his jacket. His stomach was too empty for it to hold tight. He pushed it almost up to his neck and walked on.

He made it to his desk without further mishap. His intent was to hide his book in his desk. But Steve was there with an audience, Violet and Susan. So he couldn't.

Violet, with strings of wet hair peeking out from under her parka, and Christmas bell earrings in her pierced ears, strode up to Joey and said, "I'm going with Steve. I want to sit beside him. I want to change seats!"

"Tell her no, Steve," Joey said and walked away to the media center. He could stay in there all morning.

Reading time was not until afternoon. He could put in some last minute practice. Real practice. Not just sitting in the library with a book in front of him like he used to do all the time.

He ate lunch again with the media specialist. She never said much of anything to him. He appreciated that. But when he found a fat book to hide his Stallion book inside, she was on him in a minute.

"Hey, Joey, careful there! You'll wreck the binding!" She took both books from him. Then, as if in slow motion, she laid the big book down, keeping her gaze on the stallion book. "Hey, where did you get this book? Why, I read that every year throughout elementary school!" She laughed. "I got a book reading credit for it all eight years running. I can't believe you have my favorite book when it's been out of print for years. That dates me, right? Wherever did you find it?"

"I don't date nobody," Joey said. He was thinking of Susan's notes. Then it hit him what else she'd said. He grabbed the book, stuck it up under his shirt, and went flying toward his classroom, leaving the fat book behind. If eighth graders got a book report credit on this book, well, what was there to be ashamed of?

Violet was in his seat, so he had to sit in hers. When he did, he began to giggle. He giggled and giggled and giggled. He couldn't help it. Every time he looked at the stallion book and remembered how he thought the media specialist was asking him for a date, he giggled.

Then he giggled just because his body wouldn't stop. Harry looked at him and grinned and began to giggle, too. They were getting pretty loud and Joey tried hard to stop it but that only made it worse.

The class was beginning to get out of hand and Miss Spinner had to get tough again. She made Violet get back to her own seat. She said, "And you, Joey, if something's all that funny, come to the front of the class and share it."

As he stood to go to the front, the stallion book slipped to the floor.

Miss Spinner, coming down the row, quickly picked it up. "Why, I remember this book. Where did you get it, Joey?"

It meant revealing his secret teacher and he dared not. He just grabbed it from her, clutched his stomach, and did not answer.

Harry said, "Joey's going to report on it."

The class got very quiet.

Miss Spinner said, "Then bring your book and come stand next to my desk, Joey."

Joey's legs were heavy and the little skinny book in his hand was heavy. It took him a thousand years to walk the few feet to Miss Spinner's desk.

FIFTEEN

"The pond area at the lower school grounds is infested by white rodents," Mr. Orrin's voice boomed out.

Saved by the intercom! Joey thought.

The voice continued as it always did, regardless of what was going on. "Now, a rodent is a rodent no matter what its color. I'm asking all of you not to handle those white mice." The class went wild.

Miss Spinner, with a very stern look, said, "There'll be no further interruption of Joey's reading. Continue, Joey." Even Bruce settled down immediately.

It didn't matter. Joey didn't need more time or he'd die. He needed to start. He opened the front cover of the book. His fingers couldn't manage the pages. It seemed that they were stuck to the title page. Finally a page turned. The room grew so silent his finger across the top of each sheet sounded like the crunching of celery. Or like the sound of papers when the TV newsmen held their scripts too close to the microphone. Maybe he should pretend to be a newsman. He looked up at the class and froze.

A thousand eyes looked at him unrelentingly, concentrating on his mouth. But his lips would never move. A thousand ears strained to hear if words came out wrong. He gripped the book as he would have another time, ready to throw it or rip it and say something mean and loud. But he willed otherwise. He had to risk reading.

Miss Spinner got up and took the book from his hand. "Class, can you all see the picture?" She flashed the book all around. *"Tell* us what the book is about, Joey. Maybe you would like to read to us another day."

Susan ran up and took the book and said, "I'll help you, Joey. You can nod if I'm reading it right."

Joey grabbed the book from her hand, flipped to the right page and opened his mouth, but words would not come.

Miss Spinner stood right next to him and Susan ran back to her seat. Miss Spinner whispered, "Nothing—"

In a high voice Joey heard himself say, "Nothing—"

Miss Spinner whispered the next word, "could."

The little high voice said, "could."

"Stop," whispered Miss Spinner.

"Stop—" said the tight voice and then it broke loose! The rest of the words came rolling out of Joey like gumballs from a gum machine, when a stuck penny was freed. "Wild Stallion," he shouted. Then continued on, "He fought the heat. He fought the blizzards. Now he must fight the mighty Missisisippi!" Joey read on until his five pages were done. Then he read another page to make up for Miss Spinner helping. Finally, he stopped.

Wild applause filled the air!

It was true, wild applause! And he wasn't just imagining it! Everybody in the room was applauding. Well, not quite everybody. Harry and Steve were just sitting there staring and wiping sweat from their foreheads.

Harry yelled, "You weren't lying!"

Steve said, "Read some more, Joey."

Susan said, "Oh, may he, Miss Spinner? I'd just love to know what happens to Stallion."

It looked as if Miss Spinner had tears in her eyes. She just sat there with her mouth all twisted up funny and nodded her head yes. So Joey read. He was so busy reading that he barely noticed Miss Spinner get up and slip out of the room. Everyone stayed in their seats and listened. When Joey had finished the last page of his book, he looked up to see both Miss Spinner and Mr. Orrin applauding.

At the bell for closing, Joey grabbed the stallion book and shot from the room. Down the slick waxed school halls he ran straight to the reading room. At the door he shouted, "Mrs. Hewes! Mrs. Hewes! I read!"

She sat down on the rough piano stool. Her lips were shut tight and a smiled strained the corners. She folded her arms and twisted from side to side on the stool.

"Well, get up and dance if you want to," Joey said. He himself felt so good being near her, being in the center of her clutter of books. He felt like saying the pledge of allegiance or something.

She cocked her head to one side "And—" she asked.

"And there was applause! Everyone in the school likes me! They really do. I'm not lying."

"I can see you're not. Well, I'm sure your mother will be very pleased. Have you told her yet?"

"I will. I'm telling you first. Don't you care that I read? I guess you've watched lots of people learn to read."

She smiled as if remembering. "Oh, yes. Yes indeed. And I never weary of it. Now, run along. Your mother must hear your news." She reached over and swatted him on the bottom.

He loved to have her touch him playfully like that. He had felt the strength of those old hands when they had meant business. "You happy for me, Mrs. Hewes?"

"I'm happy for you. Run along. Let me be with myself."

"You ought to be happy. Miss Spinner was so happy she cried and she wasn't even the one who wrestled me down and made me start believing." Mrs. Hewes still wasn't acting wildly pleased, so he asked her again, "You're happy, aren't you?"

Mrs. Hewes removed a handkerchief with a crocheted edge from the pocket of her slacks and sat twisting it. "I'm quite pleased and happy. I am not given to crying as is your young Miss Spinner. You have learned to read as you so wanted to do. Now, I'll say no more. Just run to your mother."

He turned to the door. Her words continued. "You have the most valuable reward that could come to a person—the knowledge of achievement. I would not mar it by offering you mere compliments. Now run—" Then she held him. Held him so close that he couldn't see her face. He could have broken the hold if he'd wanted. But he didn't want. "I've never been happier in my life," she said in a voice so husky it sounded as if it was coming over Steve's intercom. So controlled. But Joey's ears were next to her fast-beating heart. "Now run, Joey, run!"

He ran. Running, running, running! Delightful, wonderful running. He never stopped until he was in through his own back door.

Mama was not home. But she was always home when he got home! She believed in that. She couldn't be gone on today of all days. Then he remembered. This was December 22. Mama was at school in conference with Miss Spinner! He wondered what they'd talk about now that he knew how to read. Then he remembered another thing: Mama was so sure that he could read all along, she would not be impressed. It seemed impossible that he'd fooled his own mother all these years, but it was true. She herself did not read at home. There were no books in their house. No cause to shout. No cause to puff out your chest and brag a bit.

Joey needed to do just that. And it would take someone who knew how awful it felt not to read to really preen and prance with him. Joey knew just the person. And that person had believed in him all along. "Mr. Wiley! Mr. Wiley! I can read!" Joey shouted as he dashed across the backyard.

Mrs. Wiley grabbed him and hugged him hard. "Bless your sweet soul, child. A.J. said this was your big day. Oh, bless your sweet soul and a Merry Christmas to you, child." She was trembling and Joey knew it was not all out of joy for him.

"Something wrong with Mr. Wiley?" Joey was afraid to hear the answer.

"No, no, he's fine, darling. Just fine. He gonna be glad to hear your good news. He's out front working his fool head off in this weather. Don't hear a word I say. He'll catch his death of cold and us promised to go visit family for the holidays. Taking a chance in weather like this to crack that windshield again."

Joey remembered his dream of the windshield cracking still more and rushed for the front door. Outside, not only was Mr. Wiley standing there by his truck, but so was Alex. They were tightening something with lock pliers. Mr. Wiley had a *new* windshield!

Mr. Wiley saw him first. "Uh-oh," he said as he slid away from the hood on which he'd been leaning to work on the windshield. "Things not go too good, Joey?"

Alex came around from the other side of the truck wiping his hands on a rag that dangled from his belt. "Yeah, how did things go, son?"

"I read," Joey said quietly. He said it because he was too puzzled to think. Alex wasn't due home until tomorrow. Alex believed he could read all along. "I read in front of the class." He finished his rehearsed speech lamely. Then Joey turned to run.

But Mr. Wiley caught him by the hands and began dancing him about in the snow. "Bless my stars in heaven. Sure you did it! Alex, your son has done you proud. Tell your daddy all about it, Joey."

"What are you doing home?" Joey pulled away to ask Alex.

Alex was grinning. "Two good reasons. First, I found a fine used windshield for a friend of mine. Second I came home in case you blew it, reading before your class for the first time today. Believe me, Joey, I know how it is. I've blown a few interviews in my life."

Thoughts were rushing Joey. "Mr. Wiley, you told!" Joey accused.

Alex slid his arm around Joey's shoulders. "Not all I need to know, Joe. I'm afraid, just enough to get me home early. I expect you to tell me the rest."

So now he was Joe. He accepted that name from

his dad. He also forgot Mrs. Wiley's warning about catching cold standing out there in the cold and told Alex the entire story. Mr. Wiley helped. Alex couldn't believe that Joey had not been able to read at all. He'd thought Joey's problem was fear to read in front of someone. Still, he'd come home just for that! Now Joey was happy! His dad had come home just for that!

He was ready to dance circles with Mr. Wiley. He grabbed his old friend's hands. Alex said, "Count me in, too." They danced until their feet had packed down the snow so much they were laughing and sliding, not dancing. Mr. Wiley broke loose to point to his marvelous uncracked windshield.

"Good thing you didn't lay your good news on us two minutes sooner. We might have dropped our pliers and cracked it again, it being so cold and all. Alex, you sure you got this for just seventeen dollars? That's a real bargain. Any tax? I don't want to cheat you none." Mr. Wiley was taking out his billfold.

"Put that away," said Alex. "No tax at junk dealers. I found it in Nebraska, the second place I stopped. I was glad to do it. All this encouragement you been giving Joe, which I oughta been doing myself—tell you what, it's a Christmas present from me to you. You don't owe me a cent. Put your billfold away. Just stay outa the gravel pits so this doesn't happen again. Next time, I might not be so lucky."

Joey looked toward Mr. Wiley, then at Alex. He said,

"I broke Mr. Wiley's windshield. I threw a rock and hit it."

"You?" Alex was surprised. "In that case, you will pay me for it. Any son of mine makes good what he breaks."

"I was already planning to give Mr. Wiley my nine Kennedy half dollars and—"

"A. J. Wiley!" Mrs. Wiley called.

"Coming, sweetheart. We was all just ready to call time out for some hot chocolate. Wasn't we, Joey?"

"No sir. Mama'll be home by now, I guess."

"Then get skating," said Mr. Wiley. "Don't let me hold you back from so important a task as telling your Mama your good news."

That wasn't exactly what Joey had meant. But it is exactly what Alex insisted he do.

"I can read," Joe told Mama dutifully at Alex's nudge.

As soon as Mama got over the surprise of seeing Alex home early, she said, "Of course you can. I told those teachers all along—" She pulled at Joey's pants, wet about the knees and ankles. "Get these wet pants off right this minute, you'll—"

Alex put out his hand. "Chickie, listen to Joe! The pants can wait. He's telling you he just learned to read. Hey, Babe, ain't that wonderful? Tell our boy how wonderful that is."

Mama sat down. She looked puzzled and scared.

Then angry. But she didn't speak for the longest time. "Alex, the teacher gave me a good report on Joey. Don't go confusing people with crazy talk."

"Joe, tell your mama just exactly what happened today." Alex's voice was firm. "Tell your mama you couldn't read at all before this school year."

"The whole class clapped for me," was all Joey could say. He looked at his mother closely and said, "Mama, all the time you knew I couldn't read?"

"Joey, what are you saying?!"

Alex's hand reached out and touched Mama gently on the knee. "Chickie, quiet. Mr. Wiley's kept telling me what a fighter our son is. Well, now that I know what a big problem he's got past today, I'll tell the world I'm real proud of him. I want you to be, too. Look, honey, why are you so scared? I'm not going to leave you. You hear me?" He turned her face so their eyes met.

Mama had begun to cry, soft little cries from deep inside her. "I never wanted you to leave us."

"Leave you? Never! I wanted to take care of you and the kid right. Have a home nice enough for my beautiful Chickie, and for our boy. Ain't he something else, reading like that in front of his class? Aw-w-w, Chickie, baby, you didn't think I'd ditch you if I found out the kid had a problem? What's a man for?"

His dad, Alex, was holding his mama so close that Joey decided to slip into the middle of it.

"All right, son!" Alex swept him in. "Come tell us something special you want for Christmas. I'm home early. We've got an entire extra day just to shop."

Joey didn't know why he said it, or even dared say it, but being squeezed so close like he was, he did manage to say, "I'd like to go in the semi to Southern Illinois and read the stallion book to Grandma."

Mama pulled away. "Travel at Christmas time in a semi? Why Joey, you're crazy talking like that? Alex, I already got Joey a nice present—"

"Makes good sense to me. Sounds like a great way to use my extra day," Alex said. Then he slapped Joey on the back and said, "Joe's sound as a silver dollar. It's about time I met your grandma, right Joe?"

As they were pulling out for Grandma's, Mr. Wiley and Monk drove by. Joey made a triumphant O with his thumb and forefingers and Mr. Wiley waved. Monk stuck his head high so Joey saw him perfectly through the new windshield. That cat looked like he owned the world.